A
TANGLED
AFFAIR

SUBPLOT™

www.mascotbooks.com

A TANGLED AFFAIR

For more information, please contact:
Subplot, an imprint of Mascot Books
620 Herndon Parkway, Suite 320
Herndon, VA 20170
info@mascotbooks.com

Library of Congress Control Number: 2021909361

CPSIA Code: PRV0721A
ISBN-13: 978-1-63755-046-5

Printed in the United States

With love, respect, and gratitude for my mother, Emma Packett Sacrey,
I dedicate this book to my younger self, Anne Claire Sacrey.

From Philadelphia to Turks and Caicos...

A TANGLED AFFAIR

A Novel

ANNE C. SCARDINO

 SUBPLOT

Chapter 1

I was making Vince's favorite dinner, so I called to make sure he was coming home at a reasonable hour to enjoy it. I normally would have texted him because I hated to interrupt him at work, but I wanted to hear his voice. Vince ran his own international wholesale steel distribution company, so I never knew when he'd be able to leave the office.

"Hey, what's up?" he said, when he answered his cell after several rings.

"Hi, hon," I said, enthusiastically. "I'm making shrimp, pasta, and peas. What time do you think you'll be home?"

"I can probably get out of here in half an hour."

"Perfect. Everything will be done by then."

"I'll try my best. Did the tree guy come today? We're supposed to get heavy rain the next few days, and I need to make sure those two dead trees are taken down. Could do some damage."

"No, he wasn't able to come today. Said he'd get back to me."

"Try him again, and tell him he's dead meat if he doesn't get his ass over here."

"Love you," I said.

"Love you, too."

Vince took a lot of pride in our home, and he wanted everything in tip-top shape. I called the tree service but got a recording and left another message. I knew Vince wouldn't be too happy about that, so I tried twice more, to no avail.

I had about thirty minutes until he would get home, which left me time to head upstairs and change into a pair of jeans. I looked into the mirror and thought after twenty-five years of marriage, I was happy to fit into the same size jeans I wore when we first met. I worked out three times a week with Carlos, who kept me on track. I pulled my hair back into a ponytail, the same hairstyle since high school, but it still seemed to work. As I walked downstairs, I heard my cell phone ring on the kitchen island. It was Vince.

"Hey, babe," I said, anticipating why he called back. "Yes, I tried again but wasn't able to get him."

"That's not why I'm calling, but keep trying. I'm going to be late. Catherine Rogers has to go back to Los Angeles tonight, so we have to go over some things we were going to do tomorrow."

"Miss California?" I said, sarcastically.

"Clair, come on. She's doing a great job for us. She has some good contacts for possible investors."

"I bet she does. And what about dinner?"

"Keep it warm."

I was ticked. I had had enough of Miss California-turned-business consultant and Vince spending time together. I put the food in the warming drawer and turned on the local news. By nine thirty, I was asleep on the couch. I awoke to Vince banging on the side door. As I walked into the kitchen, I could see Vince standing outside the mudroom door staring through the glass panes. He never carried his key if he knew I was home. He would always leave it in his car. It seemed silly that I had to let him in, but that's what he did. I didn't say anything when I opened the door.

"Hey, hon," he said, as he gave me a quick air kiss on the cheek and walked by me into the kitchen. "Dinner ready? I'm starved. I didn't eat all day."

"It was ready hours ago."

"Sorry," he said, as he took off his coat and tossed it on the kitchen chair. "I'll eat in the family room."

"Vince, come on," I said. "I made you this nice dinner. The least you could do is sit at the table and eat with me."

"I thought you would have eaten already."

"I waited for you."

"You should have eaten."

"Well, I didn't. I thought it would be nice to eat together."

As he went upstairs to change, he said, "Not tonight, Clair, I'm exhausted. Let it go."

I didn't want to start another argument, but I felt I had to address the real issue at hand. Sure, I didn't like his eating in front of the TV, but I was disappointed about a whole lot more that had nothing to do with his watching television. Our intimacy had waned, and the issue had been addressed many times.

This was all wearing on me big time, and I had to finally do something about it before I lost my mind. Each and every day a piece of me died from not being touched. I wasn't myself anymore, but rather someone who started each day with the hope that something would happen, and it never did, leaving me down. I had begun to worry about my mental state.

I walked from the kitchen into the dark family room lit solely by the light of the TV screen, picked up the remote, and lowered the volume.

"What the hell are you doing? Turn that back up," he said,

angrily.

"Vince, we have to talk."

"Ah, geez, Clair. Please, not now," he said, as he picked up the remote and turned the volume back up. "We can talk later."

I grabbed it out of his hand and put it behind my back. "Vince, we both know that isn't going to happen. We need to talk now."

"Clair, I told you before, just be nice and things will change."

"Be nice?" I asked, as I raised my voice. "You're avoiding me, and I have to know why. I love you, and I miss being with you. For God's sake, Vince, what's wrong? Why are you doing this to me—to us? Does Miss California have anything to do with this?"

"You're crazy." He looked away back toward the television.

"Right. Just like I was crazy about our jeweler."

And then he looked me squarely in the eye. "Clair, that was a long time ago."

"Eight years, but who's counting?" I stood with my arms tightly folded.

"And you never let me forget it. That was in the past. Let's leave it there."

"We've been dealing with this same issue for years now." I could feel my voice cracking. I started to tear up, although I tried not to. "I thought after all the counseling and therapy you were going to try and change things, but you never do."

"Look, I work hard. I have a lot going on. Didn't I just take you to New York to that fancy restaurant you wanted to go to? And to the Peninsula?"

"Yes, you did, and I loved being there, but being in a gorgeous place doesn't make up for your not touching me."

"Clair, Clair," he said, brushing me off. "Stop it. You're making a fool out of yourself."

"Oh, yeah, you have that right," I said.

"Clair, I make a nice living for us. I need to expand the business, and I'll be meeting with Catherine a lot. I'll probably need to go to Los Angeles next week, or she'll come here. It all depends on her daughter."

"What does her daughter have to do with anything?"

"Her daughter is a really sweet nine year old, and she's a single mother. She's trying her best."

"You've met the daughter?"

"Yeah. I actually watched her one night in Los Angeles when Catherine had a school meeting to go to."

"What? That is so not right, Vince. You're crossing the line."

"I was out there on business, and I had nothing to do that night. She mentioned she was in a jam with having someone watch her, so I said I would. We actually had a fun time."

"How about that," I said in disgust.

"Look, let's not fight. Why don't you come talk to Steve with me? I have an appointment next week, and you can ask him anything you want."

"And what is your urologist going to tell me that your GP hasn't already told me when we met with him? 'Vince works hard, Clair; he's your typical Type A entrepreneurial guy who can't slow down. He's tired and under a lot of stress.' What about my stress? Do you or your doctor care about that?"

"I can't answer for Steve. Just come with me."

In frustration, I just stood there, hoping for him to give me more.

Finally, he said, "I love you. You know that."

I looked at him, silent, after he said he loved me. It was the "I love you" that reminded me of the early years when we married during college and were madly in love and couldn't bear to be apart. I wistfully thought of those days.

I bent down next to him and put my arms underneath his. "I love you, too. And I want to be close to you. I can't live this way. I can't take it, Vince. Something has to change."

"Okay, okay. We'll figure it out." He ran his hand through my ponytail and kissed me softly, and then with over-exaggerated passion, he laughingly said, "Can you give me back the remote now? Please?"

I tossed him the remote as I got up from the sofa and went upstairs to read in bed. At least I had a good book, but I found it difficult to concentrate. I fell asleep but got up and turned off the lights when I awoke to Vince coming to bed. He settled in, pulled the covers up, and said, "Did you try the tree guy again like I asked you?" I was turning the lights out in the bathroom, and before I had a chance to reply, he was fast asleep.

Chapter 2

I tried not to dwell on last night's exchange and awoke with a new resolve—to stop complaining about Catherine Rogers and see what might unfold at next week's visit with Vince's urologist. Steve was more than just Vince's doctor. They were close friends and played a lot of golf together, so maybe something could change. I'm sure it would be embarrassing for Vince to have to tell Steve in front of me that we weren't having sex, so maybe he really wanted to change things. I had to believe that. I wanted to believe that. Maybe this time would be different. I put on some great music—Lionel Richie—and got ready to drive to the shore to meet with my kitchen designer for a house I was developing, although the weather was horrible.

After taking a container of my homemade meatballs and sauce from the freezer, I walked from the kitchen to the mudroom and into the garage. Vince's precious Porsche was in the far bay of the garage; it was his pride and joy.

It was difficult to see the road. The Atlantic City Expressway was deserted. KYW reported that the rainstorm was hitting the South Jersey beach towns with a vengeance. The wipers spread clumps of ice across the windshield from the pounding sleet. The drive to the shore on a freezing cold day wasn't fun, but there was a feeling of inner peace every time I went to the beach where I had some of my fondest memories.

The first time I went to Ocean City was with two high school girlfriends to apply for a summer job after graduation. We were seniors in high school, and we wanted to be waitresses. I couldn't believe my parents would allow me to be away for the entire summer working at a restaurant-hotel where twelve girls lived in two small rooms with three sets of bunk beds and one bathroom.

But that was a long time ago, way before I became a real estate developer. I was working on a seven-bedroom Nantucket-style oceanfront house, and Ben Johnson was the best kitchen designer to create my vision.

I parked in front of Ben's showroom and tried not to step in a huge puddle, but it was impossible to avoid.

"Do you need some help carrying in anything?" asked Ben from the back of the showroom as he quickly got up from his desk after seeing me struggle with the door. The bright lights of the showroom were a welcome sight.

"No, thanks. I think I've got it." Water dripped from my coat and umbrella. I shivered as I managed to get through the door. "This goes right through you," I said, as I pulled down my hood and tried to smooth out my hair. "How long till summer?" I asked, kiddingly, as I got myself settled.

"Can't come soon enough for me," Ben said.

He was an average-looking man with carefully parted, light brown hair, brown eyes, and a thin build. He wasn't a man you'd notice if you were sitting on a train, but if he turned and made eye contact, you would see the kindness in his eyes. There was a gentleness that came through when he talked to me, and I greatly appreciated it.

"How are you, Clair? Did you have a nice holiday?"

"Oh, yeah, it was fun," I said, as I looked around the show-room to see if anything had changed. I was eager to see the new kitchen and bathroom displays. "Wow, I love this black and white marble floor," I said, as I bent down to feel it with my hand. "Walker Zanger?"

"Yes, their new 2012 line. Isn't it great? We just put this in yesterday. Your design ideas for the showroom have really helped with our customers. They love it."

"How was your holiday?" I asked. "Did you have your daughters this Christmas?"

"No, it wasn't my turn. Jane had them. They went on a cruise. The girls said they had fun."

Ben had divorced several years ago and now splits custody and holidays with his ex-wife. I heard from a friend he wasn't in the best shape emotionally when he did the cabinetry for her beach house, but that was shortly after he had divorced. I was sure that stress had something to do with it. My experiences with Ben had always been productive. Other people had told me that the problem with Ben was that he didn't turn the work over quickly enough. I never had that problem with him. My builder, Sam LeVele, told me that Ben liked working with me, so maybe that was the reason he always had everything ready. I thought he was attracted to me, but he never took it past the business relationship.

"I've got the plans." Ben held them up proudly as he waved them in his hands. It was nice to see his enthusiasm. Ben unrolled the drawings and placed them on the conference table outside his office. We worked for about two hours going over everything, and I made a few revisions.

"Oh my God, I love it!" I squealed, as we finished up.

Ben's secretary popped her head outside her cubicle.

"The house is really shaping up," said Ben. "Your design is right on. I love the way you managed to get in the Viking microwave, convection oven, and warming drawer and still have room for that killer eight-burner range."

"Thanks to you," I said, smiling.

"I don't know about that." His face turned red, and he glanced down from looking at me to the drawings.

"I'm glad the Viking pieces worked. You know how much I love that brand. I'm a Viking girl, even though most women prefer Wolf."

"Oh, is that so?" teased Ben. "Whether you go Viking or Wolf, you can't go wrong with either. This is going to be a showstopper. Do you have a buyer for this one yet, or is it still spec?"

I wanted to tell him it was under contract for $9 million, but I decided to leave the price out. "God sent this one, Ben. A lady came up to me while I was at the house last week and said she wanted to buy it. It was that simple. She and her real estate agent had the agreement signed four days later."

"Wow! Way to go!" Ben put his hand up to high-five mine. "I'm really happy for you, but I can see why she'd want to buy it. You're really something."

"Yeah, she liked what she saw, and as a result, she told me to just continue with what I was doing, picking everything out carte blanche."

"Well, everyone knows the quality of your designs, Clair. You have quite a reputation. With you as the developer and designer and Carl Whitney as your architect, it's a win/win."

"Yep, it's another Whitney-Bondi creation. Or, I should say, Whitney-Bondi-Johnson creation."

We both smiled. It was hard to believe that only eight years before I had started a real estate developing and design business.

It was an Oprah moment when Vince and I had looked at an oceanfront property for our family. I figured out what it cost to buy a lot, build a home, and then sell, discovering there was a lot of profit to be made. So, I did.

"Are you and Vince going away from this mess to someplace warm?" Ben brought me back from my thoughts.

"Oh, yeah, I can't wait. We leave next week for Turks and Caicos. Ever heard of it?"

"No, can't say that I have. Where is it?" he asked.

"Not too far from Haiti—gorgeous water. There's a lot of development going on right now, so it's very exciting. Much lower prices than here."

"Prices anywhere would be better than here," said Ben, shaking his head. "It's out of control. I don't know where people get the money to pay for these expensive second homes."

"Hey, wait a minute," I quickly chimed in. "Thank goodness they can, or I wouldn't have my business." We both laughed.

"Clair, I have to say, in all seriousness, you and Vince sure have it all," he said. "Nice family, great success. You make it all look so easy. How'd it all happen for you?"

"Vince and I married young, Ben. We were only in our sopho-more year of college, believe it or not. Vince worked and went to school at the same time. I don't know how he did it."

"I would have thought you both came from families with trust funds."

"No, that wasn't the case. But you know, Ben, I wouldn't have wanted it any other way. Those lean years were my happiest."

"Really?" he said with surprise. "With the life you and Vince live, I couldn't imagine there being any happier time for you than now. And didn't you guys take a great vacation to Italy just a little while ago?"

"Yes, it was fabulous—our twenty-fifth wedding anniversary.

We went to Sardinia and Taormina."

"Sardinia," he said, rather slowly. "Is that part of Italy?"

"Yes—one of the most beautiful places I've ever been. We stayed at this incredible place called Cala di Volpe that looks like a Mediterranean fishing village, but it's way more than that."

"Well, that's something. You two really live it up."

He rolled up the plans and put them aside. "I'll send you out these revisions when I get them done, probably next week, Clair," he said, as he walked me to the door.

"Oh my gosh," I said, as I put down my bag. "I almost forgot. I brought you some meatballs and sauce. Here you go. I made it yesterday. Enjoy."

"Wow, thank you so much. So kind of you, Clair," he said, as he smiled. "I didn't know you were a cook."

"Actually, it's Vince's mother's recipe. She makes all kinds of great Italian food. I'm not Italian, but she taught me how to make it. She actually cooks the meatballs in the sauce. My mother is Irish, and we only used Franco-American brand when I was growing up."

"We didn't even have that," said Ben. "Well, thank you, again."

"No problem. Enjoy. We'll talk soon. Bye." At that, I turned and headed out the door to my car. Thank goodness the rain had let up a bit.

No trip to the shore was complete without a stop at my favorite place in the entire world: Mack & Manco Pizza. Despite rain, sleet, or an occasional snowstorm, nothing stopped me from running in and picking up a pie.

"Hi, guys, my usual." I had run in ducking the raindrops, having left my umbrella in the car. My usual was two slices to eat there and then a pie to go.

"Hey, Clair, how ya doin'?" said Tony, smiling ear to ear from behind the counter.

All the guys knew me, even the ones who worked in the winter. The winter guys were different from the summer staff. They were the veterans who worked there all their lives. The college guys changed each summer as a new crew came in and dated the summer waitresses.

"What brings you in on an awful day like this?" Joe from the kitchen piped in. "Must be something important." He brought in a tray of fresh dough while Mike heaved and twirled a pie in the air. "You sure you aren't seeing somebody down here?" he said with a flirtatious wink.

"Don't tell everybody, Joe. Can't you keep anything a secret?" I said, jokingly.

"If I were your old man, I wouldn't let you out on the streets. Lucky guy!"

"Yeah, yeah," I said, as I pulled the two pieces closer and sprinkled crushed red pepper on top. The world seemed clearer to me from that counter stool looking out at the ocean. I could see Vince and me as teenagers walking up and down the boardwalk, hand in hand.

My phone rang, and I reached into my bag to grab it. It was Vince.

"Hey," he said, after I said hello. "Where are you?"

"I'm getting a pizza."

He didn't have to ask where because he knew there was only one place that would be. "How'd you make out?"

"Good," I said, as I pulled some cheese from one of the slices and tossed it into my mouth while I held the phone to my ear.

"What time do you think you'll be home?" he asked.

"About two hours from now. I'll leave as soon as I get the pie to go."

"I'll probably be late," he said, sounding preoccupied.

"Are you having dinner out?" I asked.

"Not sure. Listen, I have to run. I'll see you later, hon."

He hung up. I finished my pizza, paid, and said goodbye to the guys at Mack & Manco. I left the pizzeria and walked down the boardwalk to my car wondering where Vince was going and who he was seeing tonight, but he had hung up before I got a chance to ask, not that it would have mattered.

Chapter 3

I awoke the next morning to the sound of running water. I hadn't heard Vince come in after I had gone to bed, so I didn't know when he got home. My eyes tried to focus on the alarm clock to see the time. Vince was always up by seven, but it was only six. I heard the shower door open and close, and I shouted while I lay in bed, "You're up awfully early this morning. I didn't hear you come in last night."

I could barely hear his reply from the bathroom when he said, "Yeah." He came into the bedroom with a towel tied low around his waist and his hair still wet. He was a great-looking man. Italian men age well. He was striking: tall, handsome, with thick black hair. He worked out regularly and had a six-pack. I was always impressed with his great looks, and I could only imagine what other women thought when they saw him. He walked into his closet to get out his clothes.

"Listen, hon, I have some bad news," he said, as he quickly brought his clothes out from the closet. "I might not be able to go to Turks." He placed his navy-blue pinstriped Armani suit on the bed and paired it with a powder-blue shirt and two-tone blue tie.

"What?" I turned back toward him as I made my way to the bathroom.

"I have this big deal I've been working on for months, and I might have to go to South America."

"What deal is that?"

"I'm looking at buying a hardwood floor company based in Brazil. Next week is the only time they can meet. I'm trying to get the date changed, but I might not be able to. I'll know by tomorrow or maybe later today. I just wanted to prepare you in case I can't go."

"I can't believe it has to be next week. Why can't they see you the week after? And Brazil? Is that safe?"

Vince quickly tied his shoes as he sat on the side of the bed. He left the wet towel at the bottom of the bed, as well as the plastic and cardboard from his shirt. Vince's huge closet had every imaginable area for dressing, but he still put everything on the bed.

"I don't know. Listen, I have to run. Call the tree guy until you get him to come out here right away and have him clean up the yard from the storm, and call Joe about Turks and find out when we close." He gave me a quick kiss on the cheek. He walked down the stairs and shouted from the foyer, "I'll talk to you later." I heard the side door to the garage open and close.

Before I even got a chance to feel sad, the phone rang. "Hi, Mom."

"Oh, hi, Reese." Reese was a medical student at UCLA, so it was three thirty in the morning her time. "What are you doing up at this hour?"

"Studying for an exam."

"Good God. I hope you're getting enough sleep."

I worried about the girls. Emilie was a law student at Columbia, and she was always up late studying, too. They were twins—fraternal, so I never had to worry about getting them mixed up. Reese had Vince's coloring—brown hair, brown eyes—and Emilie had mine—blonde hair, blue eyes. They had gone to the same schools all their lives, including college at Princeton, but now they were each following their career goals at different universities. This was the first time they were separated. It was an adjustment for them, as well as for me.

"What's the matter, Mom? You don't sound good. Are you okay? Nervous about your speaking engagement today?"

"Dad might not be able to go to Turks."

"What? Why?" she asked.

"Seems there's a hardwood floor company he wants to buy in Brazil, and it's the only time they can meet with him."

"Dad really needs to learn how to slow down. Work isn't everything."

Funny she would say such a thing when she was a chip off the old block. Both she and Emilie always worked hard, whether it was their schoolwork or their summer jobs as waitresses.

"Well, I just wanted to wish you luck. Let me know how you make out. Love you."

"Love you, too, Reese. I'll let you know how it goes."

There wasn't time to dwell on the issue of Vince going to Brazil right then. I had to focus on my speech before my alma mater's business school about entrepreneurship. I had prepared, but I wanted to keep my mind in the right place to do a good job. Because I found myself in such a different place in my life than when I was a stay-at-home mom, suddenly speaking before several hundred people about how to have your own business and be an entrepreneur felt strange.

As I walked onto campus, I thought back to when I was finishing my business degree. I had dropped out after Vince and I married, and the twins were born shortly thereafter. Reese and Emilie were in middle school when I went back. It wasn't easy, particularly because I didn't want my returning to college to interfere with our home life. Vince finished his degrees while the twins were babies.

Today was one of those late winter days that felt like spring. You knew it was still winter, but the temperature went up to sixty degrees, making you remember what you liked best about spring. You could tell the college kids had pulled out their shorts that had been shoved under some winter clothes that had been put away for the season.

I walked up to the grand Gothic building that housed the main meeting area for events. People were getting registered, mostly women, since it was a women's group. I felt proud when the president of the university greeted me. It was through Vince that I became active in the group, since it was he who forged the relationship with the president after getting his MBA. Everyone knew Vince and his success.

"Good morning, Clair," said President Cummings, a very patrician-looking man with a striking presence. He had the ability to make me feel important just by being seen talking with him.

"Good morning to you, George," I said with a smile.

We walked past a crowd of people, and a photographer took a quick picture of us.

"That was some party Vince threw for you last Saturday night. Katherine was so impressed. I think the husbands are going to feel inferior after that bash," he said, with enthusiasm.

"Oh my gosh, yes," I said, feeling a bit embarrassed. "It was quite a surprise." Vince had thrown me an over-the-top surprise forty-fifth birthday party at the Four Seasons, complete with a fourteen-piece orchestra and five singers. It was very special, and I would remember it forever.

"It was heartwarming to see how much he loves you, Clair. You two are an amazing couple. It's hard to believe that you have been married twenty-five years."

"Yes, I know," I said. "I'm very lucky."

"By the way," said George, "How is Vince? We missed him the other night, but I know he's busy."

I didn't have the mental focus to figure out or backtrack in my mind what night he was speaking of. "He's great," I said, not getting into the reason he wasn't there, since I really didn't know.

"Well, please give him my best."

At that, we entered the large hall. The ceilings were massive, and there were leaded glass windows with huge windowsills that were made into window seats. There was a long section of tables in the center area with coffee and light breakfast fare.

"Coffee, Clair?"

"No thanks, George. I'm good." I was actually too nervous to eat or drink anything.

We approached a table marked *Reserved* at the front of the room where the two other woman speakers were seated.

"Tamela Rogers, Clair Bondi. Sheryl Meister, Clair Bondi," said the dean. We all shook hands and took a seat as Katie Matthews, a TV reporter for the Philadelphia CBS affiliate, took the podium.

"Good morning, everyone," said Katie, with a brilliant smile. "Welcome to our fourth annual Women's Business Conference. We have with us today three prominent Philadelphia women who represent a cross section of entrepreneurs: Tamela Rogers, president of Women's Way; Sheryl Meister, retired FBI agent; and Clair Bondi, owner of Maison Plage, a building and design firm for luxurious beach homes." She smiled extra wide when she said "luxurious beach homes" and flashed her perfectly white teeth.

I felt honored and glanced at Chris Reynolds, dean of the School of Business, a look-alike to France's Dominique

Straus–Kahn: silver-gray hair, mid-sixties, well-dressed, with more than just an air of success. He was twice divorced, and there was some controversy about his hire several years before regarding a scandal involving his second divorce from a prominent senator. Chris and I had a mutual respect and admiration. We had become business friends and occasionally met for lunch or dinner after a university event. There wasn't anything more to it than that, and I enjoyed his company. He gave me a wink; I shot him a smile. He was standing in the back of the room, having slipped in when the event had already begun.

I listened to Tamela first, as she spoke of her work as head of an organization that provided legal assistance to women. She was a good speaker. I'm sure she was excellent at what she did because she appeared very focused. She told some sad stories of women who needed emergency protection orders and how her organization went about helping them.

Next was Sheryl, one of the first female FBI agents in the United States, who was from Philadelphia. She was probably around seventy-five but certainly didn't look it. She was slim and wore a gray straight skirt to the knee and a gray cashmere sweater with a string of pearls. She was very put together. But she shocked me as she began to talk. She was so engaging and interesting. I could have listened to her for hours.

She told her story of how she had been interested in investigative matters as a child, relaying a funny story about her brother and finding out what he had done with her piggy bank, calling the experience the beginning of her detective work. Her career had come a long way from that day, taking her to Harvard. She relayed stories of working in a man's profession and how she had to think more like a man. She stressed the seriousness of her work, but she also talked about practical things that everyone could do to protect themselves.

"Don't judge a person by how they look and how they project themselves. Not everyone is as he or she may seem. Actions speak louder than words, and if something doesn't seem right, maybe it isn't."

I felt like she was speaking to me. I thought of Vince and his million excuses about where he was and why he couldn't go places with me.

"If you don't act upon something that doesn't appear to be right, it might be too late to get the chance to go back, resulting in major problems in your life."

I was next. After a glowing introduction about my work and success, as well as mentioning Vince's work at the university, it was my turn to tell my story.

"Good morning. Thank you for having me. I've been an entrepreneur for eight years now, and I still can't believe it." The audience smiled. I began to feel less nervous. "If I could become an entrepreneur, so can you. But you must first think like one, and that can take some time." I talked about the houses I had built and how I just innately knew what to do in building and designing them. "It's not neurosurgery, you know," I said, as I explained how it all came about.

After I finished speaking, Katie asked the audience if anyone wanted to ask a question. A young Black woman eagerly stood up. "How do you know what 'good' is?" she blurted out. The audience looked puzzled by the question and started to laugh, but I knew what she meant. It reminded me of my transition in tenth grade from a city school in Philadelphia to an affluent school in the suburbs.

I wanted to handle the question with sensitivity, and I tried my best. "It takes exposure, sort of like eating at a good restaurant with food prepared by a great chef. You develop a palette for fine food, just as you develop a palette for fine things."

"I study books to see what good things look like," said the young woman with large, very hip-looking tortoiseshell glasses. "But I can't afford to go to expensive places to taste the gourmet food or buy expensive clothes."

That went right to my heart. I remembered wearing a maroon-colored jumper I had made in home economics class on my first day at Abington. So, I suggested to her what I had done.

"Bargain shop," I said with a smile. "Find the expensive thing in a magazine and then look for it in a less expensive store. I used to drive my mother crazy looking at all the bargain shops. I was able to get the same dress my friends would pay full price for at half the price. Bargain hunting is a great skill to have. It will serve you well in life." I made a mental note that I wanted to meet this student after class. I felt like I was seeing myself in her. "Catch me after the seminar and we'll talk further. And, I know you know what good is by those fabulous glasses you're wearing," I said. "Those look great."

"Walgreens, $19.95," she said, chuckling.

"There you go!" I said, as I lifted my arm into the air. "You're already on your way." The audience laughed and clapped.

After closing remarks by President Cummings and additional pictures, I walked by some of the students waiting to talk with the speakers. The students stood clutching their books, hoping to make a contact that could get them a job someday.

"Thank you so much for taking the time to meet with me. I really, really appreciate it," said the woman who had asked me the question.

"No problem. Do you have time for a cup of coffee?" I asked. "We can go to Starbucks, just down at the commons."

"Sure," she said, with excitement. She reached out her hand and said, "I'm Ursula Johnson, a senior marketing major."

"Terrific. It's a pleasure to meet you. Clair Bondi."

"Mrs. Bondi, I so want the kind of life you talked about, although I know that it won't be anything near what you have done. But I want to have a home and support myself, which for me is a big change from how I grew up. I'm just trying to find a way to get it. It hasn't been easy, but I'm working hard to have a better life," she said, almost apologetically.

"First of all, Ursula, please call me Clair."

"Oh, sure, that would be nice," she said, a bit more at ease.

"Where did you grow up?"

"Just a few blocks from here."

Anyone who lived a few blocks from where we were was probably living in a run-down row home. It was one of the poorest neighborhoods of Philadelphia.

We got to Starbucks; she got coffee, and I got tea. We sat down to talk at the counter facing the commons.

"My mom raised me herself, but then she got into drugs, so my grandmother took over. I made a lot of mistakes going down the same road my mother took, but after my best friend died of an overdose, I got my act together. The university has a program for kids in the neighborhood who want to finish high school and then enroll. It builds a good relationship with the neighbors. We don't have a lot of role models, so it's great when we get to meet successful people like you."

This girl was amazing to have turned her life around. Ursula, though very understated in her dress and makeup, was naturally attractive. Her hair was short, which drew you to her face, particularly with her glasses.

"Are you living by yourself right now?" I asked.

"Yeah. My mother never came home after she served some time. We tried to find her, but we couldn't. My grandmother passed away three years ago, so I live in the house my mother and grandmother shared. I work at night as a waitress at the IHOP to support myself. I only have another semester, so I'm almost there."

"And after graduation?"

"I already have a job waiting with Campbell Soup in Camden," she said proudly, "in the marketing department."

"How wonderful! Good for you!" There was something about Ursula that made me want to keep in touch with her. "Let's get together for dinner one night. Are you off any nights from work?"

"Just one night a week. I would love that if you wouldn't mind. I'm sure you're very busy."

"I think, or I should say, I know, you are the busy one!"

Ursula took out a pencil and paper and wrote down her name and number for me. I gave her my card. "Wow, this card is beautiful! I love that little emblem you have on it. What's that?" she asked.

"It's a fleur-de-lis. It's French. It means flower of the lily."

"Have you been to France?" she asked.

"Yes, Paris is my favorite place."

"I hope I get to go there someday."

"I have no doubt you will," I said, trying to be supportive. "This has been really nice, Ursula, and I would like to meet sometime for dinner."

"Thanks so much, Clair."

"Sure."

As I began walking, I turned on my phone. I had it off for the speaking event. There was a message from Vince.

"Hi, hon. Look, I found out I can't go to Turks, and I have to take a client to dinner tonight in New York. Not sure where I'll be staying. Look, gotta get this call. Love you. Have fun."

My good feeling quickly soured with his message. I walked from the coffee shop to my car. Groups of college students walked by, some seriously discussing schoolwork and others giggling, making plans for later that night.

Chapter 4

I decided to spend the night at our pied-à-terre in Philadelphia, a one-bedroom high-rise apartment with city and water views, because I couldn't bear to face Vince with how disappointed I felt. The strain of our relationship was taking its toll. It was all I could think about when I woke up. All the signs were there that something else was going on. I decided it was time to face it, head on.

I picked up my handbag, opened my wallet, and took out Sheryl Meister's card. I dialed her number while telling myself to act nonchalant if I reached her.

"Hello, this is Sheryl," she said, in a warm, soft tone of voice.

"Hello, Sheryl, this is Clair Bondi. I met you yesterday at the speaking engagement at Temple."

"Oh, yes, Clair, how are you?"

"I'm good, thanks. I wanted you to know that I really enjoyed meeting you and hearing of your work with the FBI. You certainly have an interesting background."

"Oh, thank you, and I enjoyed your talk, particularly your

interaction with the young woman who asked you a question."

"Oh, yes," I said. "I actually met with her briefly after the event. She's terrific, and I want to keep in touch with her.

"It's so wonderful when we can help steer these young women in the right direction," she said with enthusiasm, the same enthusiasm she had shown yesterday. "Mentors are very important."

"Most definitely," I said, and decided to get right to the point. "Sheryl, I was wondering if you could help me out with a referral. I have someone who's looking for a detective."

"Sure. What's the situation—personal or business?"

"Personal, for a friend in the Philadelphia area."

"I would recommend Steve Madison of Madison Private Investigators. Ask for Steve and tell him I referred you." She gave me his number.

I knew I'd be busted if Steve told her why I had called, but I couldn't worry about that. I had to get to the bottom of things and find out if Vince was cheating. "Thanks, Sheryl. I appreciate it."

"You bet. Keep doing all your great designing. Really terrific stuff. I hope our paths will cross again soon."

"So do I. Have a great day." I hated that expression but found myself using it in my nervousness over what I had just done that could change my life. I dialed the number.

"Madison," said a man, rather abruptly.

"Is this the detective agency?" I asked, with some hesitation. I didn't expect a man to answer.

"Who you looking for?"

I pulled myself together and sounded a bit more confident and said, "Sheryl Meister told me to call."

"And how do you know Sheryl?"

"I met her recently. We were both speaking at an event."

"Okay. Anyone Sheryl sends my way I'm interested in hearing what they have to say. What do you need?"

"I told her it was for a friend, but it's actually for me. I think my husband is cheating, and I have to find out. Can you help me?"

"I'm the best in the business, if I must say so myself. If he's cheating, I'll find out. I do video, camera, and narrative; I tell you where he is and what he's doing. I work in tandem, so we use two cars, two people. Let me ask you first, are you ready to find out the truth? Some women aren't."

"Yes, I am," I said firmly.

"Well, you won't have too much longer to wait after we get on his tail. I'll need some information from you about him: where he works, car info, and a picture. And a picture of the woman you think he's seeing, name, etc. Can you get that to me?"

"Yes, I can." I didn't think this was going to happen so quickly. My God, I had just made the phone call about two minutes ago, and already I was getting set up to have Vince followed.

"Can you get to Jersey, right over the Ben Franklin? There's a Wawa right off of Creek Road. I'll need an advance of $5,000. If I follow him 24/7 for a week, it'll cost you $14,000. Are you up for that?"

"Yes."

"Okay, good. Usually when a woman gets to the point you are, he's cheating."

I didn't know how to respond, so I didn't say anything.

"If you can get the info I need—picture, car info, address where he works, where you live, I could meet you at one o'clock."

Although I didn't expect to meet him so soon, I decided to get it done right away. "Okay. One o'clock it is."

"I'll be in a dark blue van, Jersey plates. Just park and get in the front seat when you come."

"Okay." I felt like I was doing something dangerous.

I took a deep breath and started getting the information together. I went onto the computer and downloaded a picture of

Vince and me from a recent trip to Italy. I printed it out, as well as some online photos and information about Catherine Rogers. I didn't, however, print out her swimsuit photos from her Miss California pageant. I had all the information about his cars, as well, so I was able to print out the license plate numbers. I would have Steve follow him from his office. He would most likely have the Range Rover, but I never knew when he would take the Porsche.

Just as I was getting the information together, Vince called. "Hey."

"Oh, hi. How was New York?" I asked.

"Oh, the usual, nothing too exciting. Hey, I talked with George, and he told me you did a great job at the speaking event. He said it went really well."

"Oh, yeah, it was good. There were a lot of nice people there. I met . . ."

"Listen, have to take this call. Let's have dinner tonight. I'll call you—someplace nearby."

With what was going on at the moment, I didn't really feel up to it, but I pulled myself together. I couldn't tip him off. I jumped in the shower, blew out my hair, and put on some makeup. I had all my information ready for Steve, and I drove over to where we had planned to meet. I started to worry about someone seeing me there, even though I never stopped at that Wawa.

I made good time. I was fifteen minutes early, and I spotted the blue van parked away from the other cars as I pulled into the parking lot. I guess I should have told him I would be in a blue BMW, but I figured it didn't matter what I was driving, just that I would be able to find him.

I pulled in next to the van and got into the passenger front seat, as I had been told to do. After I got in, I thought maybe that wasn't the safest thing to do.

"Hi," I said, as I stepped up into the tattered seat, collecting several newspapers and handing them to him before I sat down.

"Hey, nice to meet you," he said. He was a dark-haired, dark-skinned man dressed in jeans and a flannel shirt. He appeared to be about mid-forties.

"I have the information." I handed a file to him as I was explaining what I had brought. "I think it's everything you asked for."

"Nice looking guy," he said, as he looked at Vince's picture. "Italian?" he asked, holding up the picture.

"Yes, 100 percent."

"Lucky you. You two must have good-looking kids." Even in this awful situation, it was nice to hear something positive. He didn't say anything about Catherine's photo, although he glanced at it longer than he did at Vince's.

He got right to the point. "Okay. When do you want me to start following him? I'm free for the next week."

"Well, we're having dinner tonight. Not sure where at this point . . ."

He cut me right off. "What about tomorrow night?" he asked.

"I'll try to find out his schedule, which always changes."

"Don't wait too long. If you want to get this done, you have to be aggressive. We'll get him eventually. Call me when you want to start. If you find a situation arises where you think he'll be able to be followed, let me know. I'll start when you want me to. But when we do, we need to follow him for seven nights straight. If he's seeing someone, he won't be able to wait more than a few days to see her. Most men see the woman at least twice a week."

"Okay," I said, as difficult as that was to hear. "Is that all for now?" I just wanted to get out of the truck.

"Just the check for the five grand to get started."

"Oh, yes, I have it made out already." I handed it to him, got into my car, and left. No sooner had I left Steve and began driving toward the bridge than Vince called. I nervously reached for my phone. "Hello," I said, acting like I didn't check to see who it was on the caller ID.

"Hey, babe, sorry to disappoint, again, but plans have changed. I'll make it up to you this weekend. I have a guy coming in from Bucks County for dinner. I can't get out of it."

"Oh," I said, and decided to try and get some information. "Who are you meeting?"

"You don't know him."

"Where will you go for dinner?"

"Not sure." He was never sure.

"Okay. I'll be at home," I said and hung up.

I drove over the bridge and pulled off to the first place possible and got out Steve's card and dialed his number.

"Madison."

"Steve," I said, "It's Clair Bondi."

"What's up?"

"I think you should follow Vince tonight after work. He just called and changed our dinner plans. He told me he's meeting a guy for dinner, but he was nebulous about it."

"Sounds good. I'm free and have another detective who can work it."

"Can I call you later to see what's going on?" I asked. "Or if you find out anything?"

"I don't work that way. We'll call you if we get him definitely on the first try, but we have to have solid, clear evidence to get him in one shot. There's no way of knowing. If we get the two of them checking into a hotel and coming out a few hours later then, sure, we got him."

"All right, but please call me as soon as you find out anything. I'll be home waiting."

I drove back to Villanova. I started to feel nauseous, although

I hadn't eaten anything. I changed out of my jeans, put on my flannel pajamas, and collapsed onto the sofa in the study. I put on the television. I was listening and watching, but all I could think about was Steve following Vince. I was beginning to regret my decision to involve the detective. I reached for my phone to call him but then decided not to.

Several hours passed. It was eleven o'clock. I couldn't stand not knowing. I wanted to call Steve, but I knew that I shouldn't. I had to get out of the house. I went upstairs and changed back into my jeans, grabbed my coat and phone, and drove to the all-night CVS. When I got to the store, I didn't take a cart; I just walked up and down the aisles. I felt like a crazy woman. I didn't know what to do. I bought a pack of gum and some tissue boxes. I always had to have tissue boxes ready.

As I drove back home and down our lane, I saw Vince getting out of his car. I stayed back as far as I could. He didn't see me. I drove past. My God, I wondered if Steve had caught him. I couldn't take it any longer and called Steve's cell phone.

"Madison."

"Steve, I'm sorry to call, but I can't take it any longer." My hand was shaking. "You have to tell me if you caught him," I pleaded.

"Look, Clair, calm down. I know this isn't easy, but it's a process. Even if we suspect something or have some information, we have to get him a few times. If I give you the information from tonight, you might blow it."

"I can't wait to know," I said. "I promise I won't interfere, but I must know. I will go out of my mind tonight if I don't know. Please, please, I can't take it. What happened?"

"I know I'm not doing the right thing here as far as my work goes, but you pay me, so I have to take your lead. I can only advise. It's up to you."

Oh my God, he was going to tell me. I was going to find out.

"He was with Catherine Rogers. She's staying at the Four Seasons. They had dinner, and then he went up to her room for several hours. We need to stay on him for the next week," said Steve. "If he finds this information out now, he'll just say he had to go there for some reason—possibly work related. Probably say he had to drop something off."

There was silence.

"Clair, are you there?"

"Yes, I'm here. There's no need to follow him anymore. He lied about where he was going tonight, and I've been through this once before. I'm done."

"Are you sure you don't want me to continue following him?"

"I'm sure."

"Okay, it's your call. We also have the B-roll from our van that was set up in front of the office that taped people going in and out. I'll give you that, too."

Just as he said that, my phone beeped in. It was Vince. He was probably wondering where I was, since I had told him I would be at home. I quickly got off the call with Steve and answered, trying to sound like nothing was wrong.

"Oh, hi," I said.

"Where are you?" he asked.

"I decided to go back downtown. Sorry I forgot to let you know."

"Okay. I'm exhausted," he said.

"Where did you end up having dinner?" I asked, casually.

"Oh, he insisted on going downtown."

"He?"

"John Goodwin. You don't know him."

"And where did you and John Goodwin go?" I asked.

"The Capital Grille. There were some other guys who were in just for the night who were staying in town, so we all went there.

Look, hon, I've got to get to bed. I'm exhausted. Talk to you tomorrow." He hung up the phone.

All lies. Nothing but lies. My head was pounding as I drove back to the city. I don't remember driving into the parking garage. My life with Vince as I knew it was over. There was no going back.

Chapter 5

I awoke the next morning to the sun beaming through the window. For a split second I thought I was still in my previous life, but then the horror of last night kicked in. My face felt puffy from crying.

So, it was Miss California after all. She was so young. She couldn't have been more than twenty-five, a whole twenty years younger than I. What in the world could she have given Vince that I hadn't, other than a killer body and the recognition of Miss California?

As upset as I was, I knew this was it. I had to leave. The girls would be devastated, but they had to know. I would have to tell them about the first affair so they would understand why I had to leave. I would figure out a way to tell them. But I couldn't dwell on that at the moment.

I went into the bathroom and looked in the mirror. Because I had slept in my makeup, my mascara was all over my eyes. My lipstick was all over my lips. My hair was sticking up every which way from tossing and turning all night. Who was this person staring back at me in the mirror? I hated the way I looked, and I hated the way I felt. I wanted to be happy.

My phone rang, and it snapped me out of thinking about myself. It was Chris.

"Hello," I said.

"Hey, you," he said, while drawing out the word *you*. "You slipped out on me at the conference, and I didn't get a chance to tell you how amazing you were."

I started to tear up, and I couldn't get any words out. I knew I shouldn't share this information with him, but I couldn't contain myself.

"Clair," he said. "Clair, are you there?"

My voice started to quiver, but I managed to get out, "Chris, I found out that Vince is cheating on me."

There was a pause, and then he said, "What do you mean, Clair?"

"Vince. I caught him. He's running around with a consultant from California, Catherine Rogers. Do you know her?"

"I have met her," he said, reticently.

"Chris," I pleaded, "did you know they were together? I mean, like his mistress?"

"Clair, I don't know what to say."

"Chris, you must tell me."

"I didn't want to hurt you, but at the same time, I want you to realize that a lot of people knew about them."

"A lot of people? Like who? Everyone knew but me? How could people condone such a thing? Why didn't anyone tell me?"

"Money. It's all about money, Clair. Vince has money and power, and you guys donate heavily, so no one wanted to upset all of that. What are you doing right now?"

"Oh, God, I'm a mess. When I found out, I couldn't go back to

Villanova, so I told Vince I'd be in the city. I can't go home. I'll just stay here tonight. I feel like such a fool."

"You aren't a fool, Clair. You're a kind, sweet woman who loved her husband, and he didn't appreciate you," he said reassuringly. "Look, why don't I stop by tonight. We can talk. You're going to need some support. You shouldn't be alone."

"I don't know. I have so much to do. I definitely want a divorce. I need to go see a lawyer."

"Are you sure about that?" he asked.

"Yes, I'm sure," I said, without hesitation. "It's happened before."

"Then there's only one lawyer—Lynn Gold Biken, the 'Ball Buster,'" he said, from experience.

"You're right. I have heard that she's the best. I'll make an appointment. I just don't know how long I can put up this façade. I want to tell the girls first."

"You will. You're a strong woman, Clair. You're smart, and you'll get through all of this."

"I don't know."

"I'll call you a little later. I can get out of here around seven."

Chris was right. I needed support, and he was good for me.

I called Lynn Gold Biken's office and made an appointment. The earliest available was in two weeks, so that was what it had to be. There really wasn't anything else I could do at that point. I decided to still take the trip to Turks with the girls and deal with it all after the trip. I needed to call Vince and tell him I was staying in town tonight. I didn't want him to know anything else. I checked my email, and there were messages from my tennis group asking where I was yesterday. With everything that was going on, I totally forgot my weekly match.

There was only one person, my childhood best friend, Barb Elston, who knew my real situation with Vince. I wanted to call her but couldn't handle doing it right then. Barb married a New Jersey politician, had four great kids, and lived a lovely life with many friends in the charming community of Haddonfield.

I was about to get in the shower when Emilie called.

"Hi, Mom!" said Emilie with great enthusiasm. "I can't wait until Turks! I just bought some self-tanner. What's the plan? Just the usual stuff? I just talked with Reese, and she said that Dad might not be able to come because of business."

"Oh, hi, Emilie, so nice to hear from you. Yes . . . yes . . . Turks . . . right . . . yes, the usual. Ah . . . dinners, the like . . . you know . . ."

"Mom?" she asked, sounding puzzled. "Are you in the middle of something? You sound distracted."

"Oh, no . . . just busy getting things together."

"Where are you?" she asked.

"I'm in the city, and I'll be here tonight." I wanted to make sure she knew that in case she spoke with Vince later.

"Okay, good, good. Gotta run. Try to make sure Dad changes his plans. See you in a few days. Love ya."

"Love you, too, Emilie." There wasn't anything more I could do at the moment. Chris would come over later, and we would talk. I was actually feeling a bit better. I had a plan for going forward, and I knew I, like so many other women who had cheating husbands, would find a way to move on.

Chapter 6

Chris came over around six that evening. I was shocked when I opened my apartment door and saw him with a bag of food and a bottle of champagne.

"I decided you needed to just put your feet up and forget about everything. That's my goal for you tonight—just put everything out of your mind and take a break. A lot is going on for you right now, and you're going to have to take it day by day."

"But I thought we were going to talk," I said.

"We can talk, but I want it to be all positive about how you're going to get out of this mess and move on with your life. And you will get out of it, I assure you."

"Okay," I said, as he uncorked the champagne. He made it all sound so simple. I looked into the shopping bag from DiBruno's. It had cheese, olives, almonds, shrimp, hummus, pita bread, and some chocolates. "I love all this stuff. How did you know?"

He handed me a glass of champagne and made a toast. "Here's to the first day of the rest of your life. I know that's overused, but it's true."

I started to put the food out on the counter, but he insisted that I sit down. I sat on the barstool and watched him. "You're something," I said. "Were you always something?" Even though Chris and I were business friends, I had never gotten into his personal life. We both had left that out of the conversation, strange as that may be, so I was especially interested.

He smiled and said, "I was pretty spoiled, actually. Looking back, I was a brat. I had a lot of people doing things for me— nannies, valets, and housekeepers. My parents weren't around much, but everything was done in grand style. My Greek mother was a socialite and walked around like she was always ready for a big charity event."

Since I didn't grow up that way, I found his description of his life to be fascinating. "And your father? What was he like?"

"My father was British and became a shipping magnate when he met my mother. I grew up in Greece—a home in Athens and another in Santorini—but we had an apartment in London and one on Central Park, as well."

"Wow," I said. "Now I know where you got your great sense of style."

"It may sound great, but there wasn't any real home life. My mother never got me off to school, and I rarely saw my father. I was really on my own. I was a screw up, actually—a rich kid who was a brat, but I got by. I usually got what I wanted and I could fake it a bit, but I was a good student when I applied myself."

"Any siblings?" I asked.

"A sister who lives in Carmel—married to a pro golfer. We see each other every once in a while. She's ten years older than me, so she wasn't around much. Her husband is challenging, so it isn't so easy. I try to make the best of it."

"So, tell me about your wives," I said, with added interest, as

I took a sip of champagne and leaned back on the barstool. I was starting to feel more relaxed. He stood in front of the kitchen island, facing me, and filled me in.

"Well, I was married the first time right out of college. I met Margo my freshmen year at NYU, and she was the sweetest thing I had ever met. She was from the South, so she had this gentility about her that you don't see in New York City. She stole my heart, and I went after her big time. Although she was very bright— English major—she wanted more than anything to have a great home in North Carolina and raise a family, which we did—two boys, Grant and Emerson."

"I can't believe I never asked about your children. I didn't think you had any."

"The boys are great. They're both married to terrific women, and each has a son and a daughter. The boys are close, and they have a business together in North Carolina, an investment company. They love the South like their mom does."

"I assume she's there, too?"

"Yes. They're all very close. She never remarried, which I find hard to believe. Margo could have had anyone she wanted, but I think I might be the reason she hasn't gotten involved with anyone."

"How so?"

"I wasn't the best husband, and I caused her a lot of grief. I don't think she wants to risk going through another potential bad situation."

"So, for the real question, why the divorce? What grief did you shell out?"

"Well, I told you I was a screw up, and that followed me into my marriage. I ran around; it's as simple as that. I would get caught, and I would lie—your typical affair thing. She finally had enough and left me. It was a big shock to my ego. I never thought she would really leave. She was so into the family thing. It was a big lesson to learn, and I finally learned it, but it was too late."

"And number two?"

"Well, you know the whole story with that, since it was played out in the media. I got involved with Kathryn Meyer, Senator Meyer from Virginia, that is, when I was assistant dean of the Business School at Georgetown. I met her at a reception at the French Embassy. She was married, and I certainly knew that, but I didn't realize the fallout from her Italian husband."

"So, is it true that he found you two having sex?"

"Yep, it's true, and it was awful. There was quite a scene. He exploded, went crazy, throwing things, hitting me. She had to call the police. It was all over the papers. What a mess. It'll always be a mess. I didn't know if I would ever get hired by a university again, but luckily I was able to land in Philadelphia."

"So, how did the marriage come about?"

"I knew I had to marry her, and she pretty much insisted on it after the mess we found ourselves in."

"So, what was Kathryn like?"

"Night and day from Margo. She was into herself—her career. She couldn't have cared less about making a home, like Margo did. I was impressed with her, and a lot of people were quite impressed that I was married to her. I was in it for all the notoriety."

"And how long were you married to her?"

"To Kathryn, two years, and we both couldn't stand it any longer. It was a mutual split."

"And to Margo?"

"Twenty years."

"And now? Are you involved with someone now?"

"Yes, I am. Melanie Hartsfield, a CNN correspondent."

"Oh my gosh, I know who she is," I said, enthusiastically. "I see her on TV all the time. She's good and very attractive."

"The good news is she's based in London, so it's all dessert when we get together. I could never be with anyone 24/7. So, for now, who knows, but things are going quite well. She gives me space."

"So, what are your thoughts now, after having been through two marriages and now in another relationship?" I asked.

"Good question," he said, as he shook his head from side to side. "I think I now know real value when I see it. I had it with Margo, and I blew it. I didn't have it with Kathryn, so I didn't really miss out on anything when that marriage ended. I know Melanie has good character."

After he said that, he moved over and sat on the stool next to me and took my hand, looking into my eyes. "You are value, Clair—not just value; you bring energy to every situation. You make things more exciting. Bottom line: people like being around you."

It was really touching. His eyes showed sincerity—tender, staring at me with a bit of shyness. "Gosh," I said, still holding onto his hand. "That is quite a story."

"Everyone, Clair, has a story."

"I know this will sound strange," I said, "but I've been so naïve about so many things. I always thought if someone were well educated and had a great position that their personal life would be on par with that. But I have found it isn't always the case."

"You're right about that," he said, as he got up from the stool. "I didn't want to face all this myself—I mean, looking at my role. But after many years of therapy, I was forced to see my role and my responsibility in my choices. So," he said, enthusiastically, as he stood and clapped his hands in the air. "You, Clair Bondi, are an exceptional woman, and don't you ever forget it. You're really an anomaly for someone your age. Most women today as successful as you are are more demanding of their husbands and don't put up with a lot of crap."

I knew he was right but ignored his comment. "Are you leaving?" I said with some surprise and disappointment.

"Yes. I'm going to let you get some rest. So, what's the plan now?"

"Well, I'm staying here tonight. I can't bear to be with him. He has tennis and dinner tomorrow night with his weekly group. He's never missed that in ten years, so I know where he'll be. The girls will come the day after tomorrow, and we'll leave the next day for Turks. Vince isn't coming with us; he'll be in Brazil. But now I really don't know if that's where he's going or not. He might be going somewhere with Catherine. I guess it really doesn't matter at this point. I'm just going to go to Turks and enjoy the girls and face this mess when I come home."

"Good," he said, as he walked into the powder room. I got up and started putting the food away. He came out of the powder room buttoning the cuffs of his shirt.

"I'll talk to you tomorrow," he said. "Try to get some sleep." He gave me a gentle, long hug.

"You're the best." I was so grateful to have seen him that night. He gave me a lot to think about.

Chapter 7

Since I had turned my phone off when I went to bed, I avoided talking to Vince when he called the next morning. There was a voicemail from him that came in at around seven from our home number. It was now eight. It sickened me to listen to it. It said that he missed me last night and that he had come home early and fallen asleep on the sofa after having eaten a pizza. He could have been out with Catherine for all I knew, but it didn't really matter at this point.

I had to call Steve to meet him and get the tapes, which I did. He was a decent guy and only charged me $5,000. Five thousand dollars was still a lot, but at least I didn't have to pay the fourteen. I met him at the same spot, and he wished me well. I put the two tapes in my bag and drove back to the city.

I decided I needed to do something constructive. I thought it might be a good idea to try to meet with Ursula, the Temple girl, to take my mind off things. I called to see if she might be free later. We decided to meet for dinner at a local casual spot. I would call

Chris later and fill him in.

I needed to begin packing for the trip but decided to stay away from Villanova. I'd go back tomorrow. I couldn't go back today. I would send Vince a text saying I was staying in the city. With all his "activities," I was sure he didn't care if I were there or not, even though he put up a good front acting like he missed me when he texted.

There was an email that came in later that afternoon from Chris asking how I was doing and one from Vince saying that he would be out with his tennis group later. I changed my shoes and walked to Farmicia, a homegrown foods restaurant that had great healthy food, where I was to meet Ursula. She was able to take the bus from school.

"Hello, hello," she said, as she gave me a hug. "You are so kind to meet me. I know how busy you are."

"I'm not that busy," I said.

"I just came from class. I have a lot of work to do for my senior project."

"I'm sure it will pay off," I said, with certainty.

"Clair, you're amazing. I was so in awe of you when you were speaking at Temple."

"I'm glad that I could shed some light on what it means to have a business."

"Oh, for sure," said Ursula with excitement. "But the part I loved was when you talked to me and answered my question."

"That was quite a question, Ursula. I think a lot of women may have been wondering the same thing. As you get more experience, you develop a reference point of knowing how and what to expect. You figure it out."

"I can't wait to figure it out myself!"

Ursula was a gem—so sincere and wide-eyed. She reminded me of myself in many ways.

I decided to delve a little deeper into her personal life to see if there was anything I could help her with. "Ursula, how do you keep it all together with all that you have been through with your mother's drug use and even your own drug use? That must have been very difficult to overcome."

"Well," she replied, "I couldn't go anywhere but up because I had reached rock bottom. I also have something that haunts me every day that I'd like to tell you about."

"Oh?" I said, looking a bit puzzled.

"I have a child, or at least I had a child. A baby girl I gave up for adoption. I was sixteen and didn't know what to do. I think about her every day. I still can't shake it." She put her head down a bit.

She threw me off guard. I found it shocking to think of what she had been through giving up her daughter and the emotional toll it must have taken on her. I tried to be supportive. "I'm sure you made the right decision under the circumstances. Would you ever consider trying to find her? People do that all the time. With all the computer searches and things today, it could very well be possible."

"When they took her from me, they told me I would never be able to find her."

"Well, they may have said that, but that might not necessarily be the case. I could help you look into it, if you decide you might want to."

"I hadn't considered that because I didn't think it was possible. But now, I'll think about it. You make everything sound so easy."

Little did Ursula know what I was dealing with, but I wasn't about to get into my personal life.

We talked for another hour, and it was delightful. Ursula definitely lifted my spirits, and I told her what a great person she was. Obviously, she wasn't used to such positive reinforcement, but she seemed to welcome it. We decided to meet again soon.

I walked back to the apartment and thought about the girls coming home tomorrow. Reese would be home early, taking the red-eye back, and Charles, our driver, would pick her up from the airport. Emilie would take the train and be home before noon, and we would have dinner that night at the club. I wasn't looking forward to facing Vince, but I knew I had to. The thought of spending time with the girls, regardless of the horrific stuff that was going on, made me feel better.

I feel asleep in my clothes on top of the duvet cover and slept soundly all night.

I was up early the next morning. The phone rang at 6:23 a.m.

"Is this Mrs. Bondi?" said the husky male voice.

"Who is this?" I said, not wanting to give out any information to someone I didn't know, especially at that hour of the morning.

"This is Captain Martin of the Philadelphia Police Department. Are you the wife of Vincent Joseph Bondi?"

"Yes, yes," I blurted out.

"You need to get to the Hospital of the University of Pennsylvania as soon as you can. Meet me at the ER. I'll be waiting for you."

"Oh my God, waiting for me?" I said, my voice quivering, "What's wrong? What has happened to Vince?"

"Mrs. Bondi, is there anyone you can bring with you, a family member or friend?"

"Bring with me?" I said in fear. "What do you mean? No, no, there isn't. I'll jump in a cab. Oh my God! Oh my God! Why won't you tell me what has happened to my husband? You must tell me.

Is Vince okay?"

"There's been an accident. Just come as soon as you can. I'll explain when you get here."

I knew this was serious. I called Barbara. Her husband, Jack, answered, and I started screaming into the phone that I needed her at the hospital right away. He said they would both come as soon as they could get there and that they were leaving immediately. I called the front desk and had them get me a cab. I grabbed my bag, not knowing what I was about to face.

Chapter 8

The cab driver listened when I told him to floor it. We got to the hospital in record time. Media vans and police cars flanked the entrance to the ER. *Dear God in heaven, please let Vince be okay* were the words I kept saying over and over in my mind. Vince's cardiologist stood at the door, along with a police officer, as I raced from the cab.

"Joe! Joe!" I shouted, as I approached the door.

"Clair, come with me. This is Captain Martin," said Dr. Joseph Conti, chief of the department of cardiology. I made eye contact with the captain, but focused on Joe.

I was sobbing uncontrollably. "Joe, please tell me what has happened. Is Vince okay?"

He ushered me into a room off the main area and closed the door.

"Clair," Joe said, as he held my quivering body. "There was a shooting." He then held me tighter and said, "Vince was shot in his car along Cobbs Creek Parkway. He didn't make it, Clair. I'm so sorry."

I was told that I screamed and fell to the floor, but I don't remember. The next thing I did remember was waking up in a hospital room with Reese by my side. Her face hovered over me, looking down with swollen, red eyes. Her mouth quivered as she spoke, and it came back to me why I was there.

"Mom, Mom," she said, as she saw me open my eyes. "I'm here, Mom."

I started to cry. We hugged, and the pain was indescribable. My head felt like it was going to crack in half.

"When did you get here?" I asked, trying to compose myself. "What time is it?"

"It's a little after nine in the morning, Mom. Barbara called Charles, and she came with him when he picked me up from the airport. We're going to pick Emilie up from the train in just a few minutes."

"Does she know?"

"Yes. I told her. I didn't know any other way to handle it since she could find out before she got in, and I didn't want that to happen."

"Yes, you're right," I said, as I tried to prop myself up in the bed. Reese helped straighten my hospital gown, which was twisted around my shoulders.

"Dr. Conti's in the hospital, and he wanted me to let the nurse know when you were up. I'll go tell her."

Reese left the room. I still didn't know all the details. My thoughts quickly turned to fear that Catherine might have been with Vince, but I knew that he never deviated from the weekly tennis night, so I was hoping that had been the case. Before I could think about it any longer, Reese came back into the room.

"Reese, do you know everything that's happened?" I asked. "Was anyone else in the car with Dad?"

"No one was with Dad."

"Reese," I started to say, when Joe entered the room.

"Mom, I'm going with Barbara and Jack to get Emilie. I'll be back."

Reese left, and Joe walked over and sat down in the chair next to the bed.

"Clair, are you okay?" he said, as he placed his hand on my arm. He looked exhausted, yet still in full control.

"Joe, what happened?"

"It appears to have been a robbery that went bad. Turns out Vince had played tennis, had dinner, and was driving home. We found out he stopped at a 7-Eleven along Cobbs Creek Parkway at about eleven and got back into his Porsche. He was found shot in the chest in his car with his wallet and phone missing just a few blocks from there. A police officer found the car by the side of the road. Not a car you find in that neighborhood. I was surprised he would drive that way home rather than taking the expressway. It's a tough neighborhood."

"Vince always drove that way from West Philly. I hated it, and I was always afraid, especially with the cars he drove."

"Well, someone may have been watching him when he stopped at the store. The police are going to want to talk to you. They already spoke to Howard, and he said it was their typical tennis night—tennis and dinner. Since I also have Howard as a patient, I have his number, and I have known for years that they played tennis every Thursday night. They both really looked forward to it and talked about it a lot."

"Good, God," I said, as I grabbed a tissue. It was heartbreaking to hear the details.

"I just happened to be on. We had done a heart transplant, so there was a team of doctors here, and I was going through the ER when they brought him in. The police had done a check on the license plate, and they told me they had contacted you and that you were on your way in, so that's why I waited."

"Thanks, Joe. I really appreciate your being here, considering the day you have had."

Even though Vince looked like he was in good shape, he dealt with high cholesterol and had undergone several heart procedures to open clogged arteries. Joe knew Vince well. We had known him for years. He was chief of the department and highly respected. He was also a very kind man.

"I wish I could have done something more, Clair. Your daughter is a trooper. Vince was so proud of her being in med school. I can see why," he said, with a smile. "Clair, is there anything I can do? I am just so sorry."

"No, Joe. You've been great. Thank you so much."

He was about to walk out of the room, when I had to ask one more question.

"Joe," I said, "how did the police find out that Vince stopped at the 7-Eleven?"

"They questioned the cashier right after they found him shot in his car just a few blocks from there. There isn't much around that area, just the park, so they went there first. The cashier remembered Vince pulling up in his Porsche and told police he had a conversation with him about it."

"Well, that makes sense. I'm sure they don't normally see anyone in that area in a Porsche."

I was beginning to get a handle on things, as tragic as it was. I was glad at least no one would have to find out about Catherine. We had all been through enough. I would protect that information at all costs. Neither the girls, nor anyone else other than Chris, would ever find out about Vince and Catherine's relationship. I wanted the girls to live the rest of their lives as they always had—believing that their parents loved them and had a loving marriage. My first task was to call and cancel the appointment with the divorce lawyer. That needed to done before I even made any of the funeral arrangements. I just wanted to get home. I pushed the button for the nurse and told her I was ready to leave. She agreed and said that Dr. Conti had signed off for whenever I was ready.

Just then, Captain Martin came into the room with a woman. I hadn't paid much attention to him when I first arrived at the hospital. He appeared very dignified and approachable, and he had an uncanny resemblance to Denzel Washington, which caught my eye. "Mrs. Bondi, I'm Captain Martin. We met when you first came to the hospital and saw Dr. Conti."

"Yes, I remember."

"How are you doing? I realize that's a difficult question under the circumstances, and I apologize for asking."

I didn't know what to say, so I just nodded my head.

"I want to introduce you to Detective Edwards. She's going to be handling the case along with me."

"Hello."

"Mrs. Bondi, I'm very sorry for the loss of your husband," said the very attractive woman around forty. She had long brown hair that fell close to the oval shape of her face, and she was tall and thin. She had on a short leather jacket, black pants, and heels. "May I ask you a few questions? I know you have been through a lot in the last several hours, but I need to ask a question or two."

"Okay."

"Mrs. Bondi, where were you on Thursday evening?"

"I stayed at our apartment in Society Hill. We have a pied-à-terre there."

"Excuse me, Mrs. Bondi, but what exactly is a pied-à-terre?" she asked.

"A small apartment in the city. Our main home is in Villanova."

"Oh, I see," she said. "So you stayed there on Thursday night?"

"Yes, that's right."

"Was your husband to come and stay there with you overnight on Thursday?"

"No, he was going back to Villanova. Since I wasn't staying there, I didn't know he hadn't made it home."

I started to tear up a bit and took a minute to compose myself. All the thoughts of why I was really staying at the apartment in the city rather than in Villanova started to surface. I wasn't going to tell the detective about Catherine and the fact that I had caught them cheating and was going to get a divorce. I didn't see any need to disclose that information. Plus, he hadn't been with Catherine last night, anyway. He had been shot in a robbery.

"All right, that is all I need to know for now. We'll be in touch. Thank you."

"Detective Edwards," I said, as she was about to leave. "Dr. Conti told me that Vince stopped at a nearby 7-Eleven. Why did he stop there?"

"Black licorice. The cashier remembered him when we questioned her, and we have the surveillance tape—but we can get into all that another time," she said.

That certainly was Vince. He loved black licorice. I actually found myself smiling, as odd as it was. There I sat, thinking about Vince driving home in his Porsche and having an urge for the black licorice that he loved. Funny how such a simple thing brought him such pleasure. He didn't care where he bought it—whether it was a gourmet candy store in La Jolla or at the counter of a 7-Eleven. It was that sort of thing that I loved about Vince. It brought back memories of the guy I had first fallen for—the simple guy who enjoyed simple things.

With that, she looked at Captain Martin as if to say that my information was sufficient to explain why I didn't know that

Vince hadn't made it home.

"Okay, Mrs. Bondi," said Captain Martin. "Get some rest when you get home. Detective Edwards and the rest of our team will do everything in our power to find out who did this to your husband."

"Thank you," I said.

As Captain Martin turned to leave the room, he looked back and said, "Oh, I need to ask you one more question. I assume Vince wore a watch? There wasn't one on his body."

"Yes, he always wore a watch. I would be able to tell you which one he had on by checking his jewelry box; actually, his electric watch winder. Vince loved watches and had several. I know he had six because that is how many the watch winder held. And they were all engraved with *VJB* on the back."

"Okay, that will be helpful to know. Thank you, again, Mrs. Bondi."

As soon as they left, I got myself dressed and waited for Reese and Emilie. I saw on my phone that Chris had called several times. I wanted to talk to him, but I couldn't right then. I knew the girls and I needed to see Vince's body in the morgue, as difficult as it was going to be.

Reese came back with Emilie. She stayed outside the hospital room along with Barb and Jack while Emilie came into the room by herself.

"Mom, oh, Mom," she said, as she hugged me tightly. Tears flowed down her face.

"Emilie, my sweet Emilie," I said, as we tried to comfort one another.

"When can we see Dad?" she asked. That was Emilie, very direct, very focused on the task at hand.

"I think right now. Are you ready?"

"Yes."

"I haven't even spoken to Barb and Jack yet. Can you send

them in for a minute before we go down?"

"Sure."

Barb and Jack came in, and we all hugged. I thanked them for all their help in getting the girls and handling things for me, including canceling our flight and hotel reservations for the Turks trip. I thanked God that I had them as friends. I surely needed them now. They offered to drive us home to Villanova, which was very nice of them. They wanted to go with us to see Vince's body, but I told them it was something the girls and I needed to do ourselves.

With that, the girls and I, along with one of the nurses, went to the elevator and down to the morgue. The nurse led the way, and we all held hands and wrapped our arms together tightly as we walked behind her and entered the stark stainless-steel room. I saw a drawn curtain that didn't come quite all the way to the floor, exposing the wheels of a gurney. I knew Vince's body lay behind the curtain on that gurney waiting for us.

We were all crying. The nurse asked if we were okay to proceed. We told her that we were. As she pulled the curtain aside, I saw Vince's body covered with a sheet up to his neck so just his face was exposed. He looked like he was sleeping. His face was just like it had always looked, except he needed a shave. *How strange,* I thought—*a dead man, but his facial hair still thought he was alive.*

As I looked at him, all I could think of was the hurt I felt with his betrayal. I couldn't think of anything else. How sad that the day after my husband died, instead of thinking of all the great times we had together, I was thinking about Catherine Rogers. Did she know by now that he had died? I was so very sad, but I was so very angry. I wasn't even the last person he made love to—that honor went to Catherine.

The girls each kissed him on the cheek and cried uncontrollably. I didn't think it was good for us to stay too long. We would have time for that at the funeral home.

"Mrs. Bondi, would you like a few minutes by yourself?" asked the nurse. "I would be happy to stay with the girls outside while you take a little time."

I really didn't want to, but I thought the girls would think it strange if I didn't.

"Okay. I'll just be a few minutes." At that they left the room.

I stood there and felt numb. Which was worse, divorce or death? I was dealing with both. *Vince, oh Vince, why, why?*

I walked out of the morgue, and the girls and I left the hospital with Barb and Jack. The ride to Villanova was awkward. Jack commented on the light traffic, but no one responded. He was trying his best to make things better. No one, however, could make anything better.

Chapter 9

We arrived at home exhausted, sad, and dazed. I called Vince's sister, Teresa, who was a big help. She and her husband and son lived next door to Vince's parents, Tony and Mary, who still lived in the house where they had raised Vince. They all worked together in a cleaning business that Teresa and Nick owned. Mary did the sewing, which she did to perfection, and Tony handled the deliveries. It kept them young. Teresa told me their family doctor came over and gave her parents a sedative. They didn't want to take it, but she insisted and said they went to sleep with broken hearts. My own heart ached for them.

My mother lived in Key Largo, Florida, with her sister Peg. My dad died of a heart attack at age sixty, ten years ago; Aunt Peg's husband, Elliott, died fifteen years ago at age sixty-five. I was dreading the call to my mom. I knew she would be upset, but I also knew she thought Vince should have been home more. Whenever I'd talk to her, she would ask me where Vince was, and if he were out with his weekly tennis group or biking in New

Hope on Sunday mornings with some guy friends, she would simply respond, "Oh." My dad came home from work every day at the same time and didn't have his own business. My dad worked and complained about his boss every night when he came home. Vince never talked about work.

I only needed to say the word "Mom," and my mother knew something was wrong.

"Clair, what's the matter?" she said, with concern. "Is everything okay?"

"No, it's not, Mom." I could feel my heart pounding. "There's been a terrible accident."

"Are the girls safe?"

"Yes, it's not the girls. It's Vince. He was driving home from tennis last night and was shot in his car. He died, Mom."

"Dear Lord have mercy," she said, sounding like she was ready to say the same line over and over like a prayer. I could only imagine her crossing herself as she said it. "Where are you?"

"I'm home. The girls are here. They were coming home anyway because we were going to Turks and Caicos tomorrow."

"Do they know who did it? Did they catch the person?"

"No. But they are pretty sure it was a robbery gone wrong."

"I'll check on flights and be up right away. I'll call Aunt Peg. She'll want to come with me. Is that okay?"

"Yes. That's fine."

There was silence for a few seconds, and then she said, "I love you, Clair."

"I love you, too, Mom."

My mind was racing, thinking of all I needed to do with planning the viewing and the funeral, not to mention talking with our lawyer and accountant. I couldn't bear to put on the radio and hear anything about the shooting. My cell phone rang. It was Chris.

"Clair, Clair. Are you okay?"

"We're all right, I guess. I mean, I don't know," I said, sounding uncertain.

"May I come by?"

"Sure. It would be nice to see you," I said, as I began to break down.

"Catherine wasn't with him, was she?"

"No, thank God. I haven't talked to Howard yet, but I was told by police that he confirmed they played tennis at Penn, had dinner at Pod, and then Vince drove home. The police have him on tape at a 7-Eleven."

"Yes, I heard that on the news. I'm so very sorry, Clair. When can I come over?"

"I need today to just be with the girls. I know a lot of people will be coming over, and I have to handle a lot of things. Oh, God, there're two news vans out front with reporters, and a police car just pulled up. I better go."

"Call me. I'll plan on coming tomorrow, but call if you need me."

"Okay."

I started to go upstairs to shower and get ready for a full day of planning the funeral and people coming over to the house when a steady delivery of flowers and fruit baskets began to arrive.

I opened Vince's closet and looked at his array of suits. It hit me that I would have to pick out his clothes to take to the funeral home. All those custom-fitted gorgeous suits were lined up perfectly. I loved the way he dressed. He got that from his mother. She was an impeccable dresser.

Calls were coming in right and left on my cell phone from friends and business associates. I let them all go to voicemail until our attorney, Bill Kaplan, called. I thought I better talk with him. He told me that both he and our accountant, Kevin Marks, wanted to see me at my earliest convenience. I told them I could meet that afternoon.

Barb and Jack came with me to the funeral home later that morning, which was a big help. I brought over Vince's clothes, and all the details were worked out. I decided to go ahead with the wishes of Vince's parents and have the high church mass and burial at the cemetery where they had plots. The girls were each going to speak.

The day was a steady stream of family and friends. Everyone was most kind and brought tons of food. Their support meant a lot. I had to excuse myself to meet with Bill and Kevin at Bill's office, which was only a mile away at the Radnor Corporate Center. Emilie and Reese wanted to come along, but I told them to stay with our guests.

Bill and Kevin were very emotional when I arrived, and we tried to get a grip on ourselves. Bill led the conversation.

"Clair, we are so sorry. There are no words," said Bill, our attorney.

"Thank you."

"Yes, Clair, we loved Vince. He was a wonderful person," said Kevin, our accountant.

"Clair, I assume you know everything about your financial situation."

"Bill, I know nothing. Vince never shared anything about our finances with me."

"Really?" he said. "And why is that, may I ask?"

"It wasn't because I didn't ask. He never would tell me anything."

"Well then, I guess we better explain some things to you." He looked over to Kevin with concern. "I know that you owned a lot of properties, but there was also a lot of debt on those properties. Based on what you just said, I suppose you didn't know that?"

"Yes. That's correct."

"Kevin, maybe you should go over the actual numbers."

"Sure," said Kevin. "Clair, you do know that you hold mortgages on four properties—your home in Villanova, the home in Stone Harbor, the place in the city, and the home in Turks and Caicos, correct?"

"Yes, I know we have those homes, but I know nothing about the financial aspects—only that I made a lot of money developing beach homes and that Vince handled all the money from those sales, approximately $6.4 million on the last four homes that I did. The only thing I know is that money was placed in an account for when I wanted to do the next project. And I also know that Vince did well because I would sign the income tax returns."

"Well," said Kevin, looking concerned, "I guess I'm just going to have to come out with it. There is no money in an account from the money that you made, and there are loans or mortgages against all the properties. If you were to sell them, on all four, there would only be in today's market about $1 million total."

I was dumbfounded. I felt like I was having a nightmare— that it was all a dream, and I would wake up and my financial life would be what I had thought it was—stable. More than stable, stellar! I felt like a bag lady, one step away from living on the streets. I knew I was overreacting, but that's how I felt. The rug had been pulled out from under me, and it felt terrible. As if the affair and Vince's death weren't enough, to now find out that the money wasn't anything that I had thought was overwhelming.

"How can that be?" I asked, in shock. "Didn't Vince make a lot of money?"

"Yes, he did, but he also had big expenses with all his projects. He had things leveraged up pretty high. I thought for sure you knew about it."

"No, I didn't. He handled the money, but he led me to believe that we were doing great. When I would sell a property, he would say, 'Could you imagine if we needed this money?' So you're saying that there is roughly one million if I sold? We're closing on Turks and Caicos in just a few weeks. It's under agreement for $2.5 million."

"Well, you'll have to pay back $2.5 million when you sell it. There's no profit on that one, but the other three, as I have said, have about a million, total."

"We're also closing on the Avalon piece. Did Vince tell you about that? We got $9 million."

"Yes, he was pretty pumped about it. You guys were lucky on that one."

"Lucky?" I asked, indignantly.

"Well, hell, in Avalon you could build anything, and it will sell; but, then again, I'm sure what you did was great." He tried to make a quick recovery to his disparaging remark.

"I know that we bought the lot for $4.6 million and have $2 million in the house, so there should be about a $2.5 million profit, after taxes."

"Clair, I'm sorry to tell you, and don't think that this isn't hard for me to say, but that money is already committed to paying off a credit line."

"Credit line?" I asked in disbelief. "What credit line is that?"

"Don't you remember signing for it? It's in both your names."

"No, I don't remember. I probably didn't. Vince probably forged it. How can this be, all this uncertainty about money?" I asked in disbelief. "I always had plenty of money in my checking account. Vince had auto deposit set up whereby I got $6,000 a week."

"Right," said Bill.

"Then why would he give me that much money when we really didn't have money from the real estate?"

"Clair, I can't answer that," said Bill, shaking his head. "And without life insurance, things are going to have to change for you with the lifestyle that you were used to living, unfortunately."

"I had just assumed there was life insurance, but rather than dealing with it before the funeral, I just paid for the funeral out of my account. Seems that I had assumed a lot of things."

"I'm shocked Vince never mentioned it to you."

"So where do I go from here?" I asked, looking for a ray of hope that this situation could be fixed somehow.

"Well, I would suggest that you sell off some of the places, and we'll try to get the rest of the business stuff straightened out. There is money there, but it's tied up," said Bill.

"How much?" I asked.

"Well, I'm not clear as to the actual number. It's a bit complicated. The business would have to be sold for you to get any real substantial money, and that might not be that easy to do."

"But," said Kevin, "the good news is that Jim has phoned me to let me know that he'd be willing to keep everything going with regard to the bookkeeping and the paying of the bills, so I'm sure that's a relief. Since he handled all the bills and the payroll for the most part, you won't have to worry about anything. He seemed broken up when I spoke to him."

"Let's go back to the thought of selling the business. What would I have to do?" I asked.

"You certainly have the right to do so," said Bill, "but I think we might be getting ahead of ourselves. Vince has his share of the business going to you, and Jim Stone owns twenty-five percent. Were you aware of that arrangement?"

"No, I wasn't. Again, Vince never told me anything about the money or how the business was set up. It wasn't that I didn't ask. I asked many times, but he'd never tell me. He just said I didn't have to worry about anything."

"We can handle looking into selling or keeping you in with a new owner, as well. It's been set up that you have full control on how you want to move forward. We can discuss the possibility further after the funeral, say in about a week or so," said Bill.

"Okay," I said.

"We'll see you soon at the viewing and the funeral. I hope you can get some rest. I'm sure you have a house full of company and friends stopping by."

"Yes," I said. "Thank you."

I was shocked that Jim Stone had ownership. It was only a small amount, but his having control over the books was beginning to concern me a bit. He could be ripping me off, for all I knew. I had thought Vince handled all of that. I drove home in shock over the real estate situation. I was glad to know at least there was money in the business, but my life was going to have to change.

When I arrived home, there was a car in the driveway that I didn't recognize—a red Mazda. When I opened the side door to the mudroom and walked into the kitchen, I saw Emilie and Reese sitting at the kitchen table with Vince's assistant, Kristee Adams, and another young woman I hadn't met. I didn't know Kristee that well, even though she worked closely with Vince, but it was only business-related things with which she assisted him, unlike other executives who have their assistants do personal tasks, as well.

"Mrs. Bondi, I'm so sorry," said Kristee, as she stood up and gently gave me a hug. Her long auburn curly hair brushed the side of my face, and her dark brown eyes stood out.

"Thank you, Kristee."

At that, the other woman stood up, and Kristee said, "Please meet Amanda Wright, one of Vince's salespeople."

"Mrs. Bondi," said Amanda, "please accept my deepest condolences. I owe so much to Vince. He brought me on board, and I will always appreciate it."

"Thank you, Amanda," I said. She looked to be around the same age as Kristee, probably early thirties. She was very thin, with a beautiful face and blonde hair pulled back at the nape of her neck. She, like Kristee, was wearing jeans.

"Look, Mom," said Reese. "Isn't this plant Kristee and Amanda brought beautiful?"

"Yes. Very nice." As thoughtful as it was for them to stop by, I could only think about my meeting with Kevin and Bill. "Hey, guys," I said. "I'm sorry, but I am so wiped. I have to go upstairs and lie down."

"Oh, of course, Mrs. Bondi," said Kristee. "We'll be on our way. We just wanted to stop and pay our respects."

"That was so thoughtful of you both." But suddenly, I had a strong desire to mention Catherine Rogers and see if Kristee knew anything about her. Everyone was walking toward the side door when I said, "Excuse me, Kristee, may I speak with you for a minute?"

"Of course," she replied. The girls and Amanda continued to walk outside. "Is there anything I can do for you?" she asked, as she walked back toward me.

"Actually, it's about Vince's funeral. Do you think Catherine Rogers will be attending?"

"Oh, Catherine, yes, CR Consulting," she said. "Maybe? I wouldn't know. Would you like me to contact her and tell her of the arrangements? I don't know if she's aware. She might want to know."

"Oh, I'm sure Jim can do that. Weren't she and Vince doing a lot of work together?"

"Yes, they were," she said. "Vince was confident that she could help to expand the business, so they were doing a lot of work on that. Did you think they were together a lot? Or, I should say, working a lot?"

"Well, no. I mean, yes. He was with her a lot, working, of course. He told me he was. I know they were working together the night before he was shot, so I just figured it was necessary, you know, the working."

"Right. I could check with Jim for you, if you want me to."

"No, that's okay," I said. "I'll talk to Jim myself and make sure everyone has been contacted who Vince would have wanted to know. Thanks again."

"Sure thing, Mrs. Bondi. If you need anything, please let me know. I'd be happy to help in any way."

"Thanks again."

As I walked upstairs to undress and put on my pajamas, I was angry with myself that I even talked to Kristee about Catherine. I should not have done that. I didn't know what Kristee knew or didn't know, but keeping the information of Vince's affair with Catherine from the girls and everyone else was my goal, and I knew that I had to be more careful.

Chapter 10

All the plans were in place for the viewing the next day before the mass and burial. I wasn't going to have the viewing the night before and the funeral the next day. I had to get it over with in one day. Vince's parents wanted the arrangements the traditional way, with the viewing the night before, but since I had agreed to have a full funeral mass, they went along with my wishes. They were devout Catholics, so the full mass with communion was very important to them.

Captain Martin called most mornings around ten with an update, but there still were no leads. He worked things out with the Radnor police to have two police officers outside my home because of all the reporters and news vans. The national exposure attracted media from everywhere.

The girls and my mom and Aunt Peg all went to get their hair done, as well as manicures. I let them all go and decided to handle those duties myself. Chris came over at eleven. When I heard the doorbell ring, I was excited. When I walked to the side door, I saw his smiling face through the glass panes, and he was holding a bouquet of hydrangeas.

I hurried to the door, but when I let him in, I pretty much collapsed into his arms. He walked me into the family room where we sat down.

"Chris, I'm so glad you're here. Thanks so much for coming."

"God, Clair, how are you coping with all of this?" he asked. He took my hands and held them tightly.

"I'm so scared, Chris, about everything," I said, with tears streaming down my face. "There're so many things, not only Vince's horrible death. I'm so afraid my girls are going to find out that Catherine and Vince had an affair. With other people knowing, I'm so worried that it's going to come out."

"No one's going to say anything to your daughters, Clair," he said, trying to be reassuring.

Just then, we heard the side door open and the girls talking with my mom and aunt.

"Mom," shouted Reese. "We're back."

"Oh, my," said my mom. "Look at this gorgeous bouquet of flowers!"

I jumped up and walked with Chris into the kitchen. Since none of them had ever met Chris, they didn't know who he was.

"Hi," I said, with Chris by my side.

"Oh," said Aunt Peg, not expecting to see me with a man, especially one so good looking. Aunt Peg always enjoyed seeing a good-looking man. Her husband had been quite handsome, and she loved that about him, as well as his kind manner.

"Everyone, this is Chris. He's the business school dean of my alma mater, and a friend, as well."

I then introduced him to everyone individually, and they all shook hands with him. He expressed his condolences and then said goodbye. Aunt Peg told him not to run off, to stay for a drink, but he graciously declined. I walked him to the side door and let him out. He said he would be at the church early the next day because he had to get on a plane to London later that night and had a lot to do before the trip. I watched him get into his Mercedes. The media outside ran to his car snapping pictures. I bet they were wondering who he was. With his good looks and the way he handled himself, whether he was speaking to a large group or opening his car door, people took notice. I stood there for a minute watching; then, Aunt Peg brought me back to reality.

"Clair, I hope we see your friend again soon. I hope he didn't run off so quickly because of us. He could have stayed, you know. I bet he would have liked some of those biscuits I baked this morning with some of that special jam I brought with me from Florida."

"Oh, no, Aunt Peg," I said. "He didn't rush off because of anything to do with you. He just wanted to come by and pay his condolences. He knew Vince because of his fundraising at the university. And I know him, as well, because of my work with the women's entrepreneurial group there."

"Well, that's all real nice, sweetie. Hopefully I'll get to see him again before I go home."

My mother was listening to all of this and just rolled her eyes. She knew how Aunt Peg went on and on about things, but they were great for one another. With my dad gone and Uncle Elliott, as well, they were good companions. They took a trip each year to Ireland, which they loved. I tried to get them to see some other countries, but they liked it there and were proud of their Irish heritage.

The rest of the day was filled with more friends stopping by. I also got a phone message from Ursula saying she had an exam the next morning and wouldn't be able to attend the mass. Before I knew it, it was time for dinner. Even though we had so much food brought to us, we all decided we just wanted a pizza, so that's what we did. There was a great new thin-crust pizza place that just opened nearby. We had it delivered and sat around and ate and drank, doing our best to pass the time.

Time—sometimes there's too much of it, and now there wasn't enough. I was feeling very sad, thinking that the girls would not have their father. They loved him. He was a powerful force that would no longer be there. He made sure that their every need was met. I felt more determined than ever that the secret I knew would remain with me for the rest of my life. The wine helped, and I fell asleep on the sofa. Reese woke me up and we both walked upstairs to bed. Aunt Peg was still up watching a Ronald Reagan movie.

The next morning encompassed a flurry of activity in preparation for a very sad day. The power went out, and luckily, I knew how to switch the circuit breaker to get things going again. The limousine was in place way before it needed to be. From my bedroom window I could see Charles waiting for us, coffee cup in hand.

I wore a black Chanel suit and my Van Cleef mother-of-pearl necklace, which was my favorite and was the last gift from Vince for our twenty-fifth wedding anniversary. But the lovely dinner and the beautiful necklace didn't make up for Vince's lack of interest in anything more that night. I vividly remembered getting into bed and reaching for him, only to be ignored.

"I'm tired, Clair," he said, with his head and body turned away from me.

"Vince, it's our anniversary," I said, as if that would have made any difference. Tears flowed down my face, but he never saw them because he never turned toward me.

Although I was forty-five, I now felt like I was sixty. My face looked old and haggard. My goal that morning was just to get through the day's events. I was hoping the time would go quickly and I would be back home in my pajamas before long.

I walked downstairs. My mom had made coffee and put out some bagels, but no one wanted anything to eat. I couldn't help but think of how beautiful the girls looked and how Vince would have been so proud of them. I knew they were each going to eulogize him, and I was trying my best to prepare for the emotion of all of that.

We got into the limousine, and, strangely enough, all the media people were gone, which was a relief. It was a gorgeous day, and the sun was shining. The drive to the church took about fifteen minutes, and after arriving, we spent some family time alone with Vince—first the girls and me, and then the rest of the immediate family. Vince's dad was so broken up that I was worried he wasn't going to make it through. I tried to comfort him, but he was beyond grief. Vince was his idol. Both Tony and Mary loved Teresa, but Vince was their shining light. He signified success, something they never knew the way Vince did. But they were successful in my eyes because they truly loved one another, and family always came first.

After the family viewing, the other guests arrived. It took about three hours for the public viewing. I didn't see anyone resembling Catherine Rogers, so I assumed she wasn't there. I was glad she decided not to come. The real emotion came when the casket had to be closed. The girls and I did it together, and it was horrible. We all held onto one another, and I finally had to just do it. Emilie tried to stop it from closing, but Reese grabbed her and released her arm. We quickly walked to another room and waited until we were told to come back into the church.

The service was rather cold because the priest really hadn't seen Vince in many years. Even though his parents were very close with Father Ginardi, Vince hadn't gone to church much.

So most of the stories told about Vince by the priest were stories about his family, not specifically about Vince. There was a lot of talk about the church and its mission.

The girls did a great job eulogizing their father. They told of all the nice things he had done for them, like moving them everywhere they had to go with their schooling. There wasn't anything he hadn't done for them. He was a model father. They injected some humor, such as his teasing them about the guys they both dated, which was nice to help with the pain of the situation.

After the funeral, the burial was just the immediate family. Seeing the hole in the ground awaiting Vince's casket was very emotional. There were chairs set up for all of us, and as we were walking from the cars to the chairs up a small incline, Vince's dad collapsed. His wife fell on top of him trying to pull him up, and Teresa shouted, "Jesus, Mary, and Joseph!" Mary slapped his face, trying to bring him around, which worked, but it was very stressful not knowing if we should take him to the hospital right then and there. He insisted on staying for the burial, but we made it quick. The priest tried his best to finish things up swiftly, giving a brief talk about how we never know what God's plan may be. We laid flowers on the casket, and I kissed and clutched my hands around it, as if Vince could feel my embrace. I motioned for the others to give me a private moment. Even though I knew he was dead, I felt terrible leaving him there. It saddened me to think of him in the ground. I finally had to leave, and it was the hardest thing I ever had to do. Vince was really gone—forever. Mary, Teresa, and Nick went with Tony to the hospital to get him checked out, and the girls and I went to the luncheon that was held at our club.

I was relieved when the luncheon was over—all the small talk was killing me. We stopped on our way home to see Vince's dad at the hospital, but they had released him from the emergency room, so he was back at home. We drove to his place and just stopped by briefly. Mary had plenty of food out for her family, who all went back to her house after the luncheon. All the aunts and uncles and cousins came in. I wished for a moment that I were one of them. They comforted one another, and no one was ever alone. They faced everything together.

The day's events came to an end, and I was most grateful to have had my mom, Aunt Peg, and the girls by my side. They were a great help, and they got me through it. Before my thoughts could wander further, my phone went off. It was Chris.

"Hi, Clair. How are you?"

"Okay. I'm just glad it's over."

"I'm about to board my flight, but I wanted to check in with you."

"Chris, you've been so wonderful. I couldn't have gotten through this without you."

"I'll be gone for four days, but will be back in touch as soon as I return. Have to run."

"Thanks. Safe travels."

I tried to sleep but couldn't. My mind was racing—Vince's affair, his death, and the investigation—it all was ripping through my head. A chapter in my life had closed. I had buried my husband. But that chapter had really been closed years earlier, although I hadn't faced it.

Chapter 11

I was glad to see the dawn of a new day. Even though it was raining, I didn't care. I actually loved hearing the rain hit the roof. The sound soothed me. Although I was drained emotionally, I felt pretty well physically and got out of bed and into the shower.

As I was showering, a thought hit me that I had three days left with my daughters and my mom and aunt before they had to head back to their respective places. I wanted to put everything on hold and spend some time with them—some quality, fun time. I had a choice: I could sit around feeling sorry for myself, or I could take us all to New York and spend those three days with four incredible women whom I loved dearly. I chose the latter and was excited to share the plan, and I wasn't going to take no for an answer. I knew there would be some people who would never understand how I could go to New York right after Vince's funeral, but I had ambivalent feelings about his death. I was sad, but I was also very angry, which they wouldn't realize. And, I had found a way in the last few years to weave in and out of all the disappointments of Vince, finding joy on my own. For the first time in my life, I didn't care what others might think.

Before anyone was out of bed, I went online and booked the next three days with one agenda: to have fun. We all needed that. I started with Barb, whose daughter was an Emmy Award-winning writer for *The Colbert Report*. The girls absolutely loved Stephen Colbert, so I was thrilled when Barb wrote back that Amanda would arrange for us to get tickets, as well as the possibility of meeting Stephen. I knew this would make the girls very happy.

I got us a suite at the Palace with three bedrooms facing St. Patrick's. Dinner one night would be Gilt, another at Jean Georges, and the last at Per Se. *La Boheme* was at the MET, so I booked that, as well. And I couldn't resist seeing *Jersey Boys* for the third time. I knew that would cheer everyone up. We could make hair and spa appointments in the car on the drive up for Fekkai. Amazing what one can do in a short time on the computer. I was feeling empowered. I raced upstairs to wake everyone up and tell them the plan.

"Good morning," I said, enthusiastically, as I opened the bedroom doors to each room, one after the other.

"Mom, Mom, what are you doing?" asked Reese, waking up suddenly.

"Clair, dear, what's going on?" asked my mom, as she walked into Reese's room.

"Martha, is everything all right?" questioned Aunt Peg, tying her robe as she walked in.

"Yes, everyone," I replied. "Everything's going to be all right. You are correct, Aunt Peg," I said with conviction. "We're going to New York for the next three days, and we're going to have fun. And, I won't take no for an answer. So, let's get going. You have one hour. Bring clothes for three days and nights, and I'll fill you in later. Let's go!"

"Mom," said Emilie, as she sat up suddenly in the twin bed next to Reese. "You want to go to New York after Dad just died? What are you thinking?"

"Why?" I asked, sitting on the side of her bed. I put my arm around her and kissed her on the forehead. "We have three days, and we're not going to waste them. I don't know when I'll have you all together again."

"Mom, no, it isn't right. How could you possibly feel like having fun right now?" she asked pressing further, as she got out of bed and walked into the bathroom. We all just stared at one another and didn't say anything until she came out. I realized how much more Emilie was like Vince than Reese—Emilie spoke her mind and always let you know where she stood. Reese was more reserved, diplomatic, and acquiescent.

"Emilie," I said, trying to smooth things over, "let's try to get through this." I tried to convince her, but she wasn't buying it. My mom and Aunt Peg both went back to their rooms.

"Em," said Reese, "come with me." At that, she took her downstairs. I went back to my room and sat on my bed, not sure what to do. I really wanted to go, but I realized that Emilie and Reese didn't understand where I was in my life at that moment. I wasn't the grieving wife and mother that they expected me to be. I was a woman who had made a decision to finally divorce a cheating, lying husband. That decision hadn't come easily. It came with a lot of pain and trying beyond everything I knew not to have to come to that decision.

I was surprised when Reese and Emilie came into my room. "We're in, Mom," said Emilie. "I'll go," she said, with Reese looking on.

"Are you sure?" I asked.

"Yes, let's go," she said.

"Okay then," I said, with some uncertainty.

In no time, we were driving up I-95, talking and listening to some Rod Stewart. The girls were happy when I told them the Colbert plans, and my mom and Aunt Peg couldn't believe we were going to the opera. Neither of them had ever been. Reese and Emilie took care of booking appointments from their cell phones for everyone at Fekkai. For the moment, I was able to compartmentalize what was going on, what I had been through, and what I still had to face. Whatever it was, I was putting it aside for three days.

We got into the city just about noon, and I pulled into the valet parking garage of the Palace.

"Good afternoon, Mrs. Bondi," said Mark.

Vince and I stayed at the Palace whenever we were in New York, so we knew the employees, who were all so kind, by name. "Nice to see you, Mark."

"I'll take care of your bags. Please, go inside. Hello, ladies. Welcome."

I felt a feeling of relief to be in a different place from home as I walked into the lobby and approached the registration desk.

"Good afternoon, Mrs. Bondi," said Alana, the desk attendant. "So nice to see you. Will you be with us for a few days? Welcome."

I was going to have to let the employees of the hotel know about Vince's death at some point, but I wasn't going to get into it at that moment. I was grateful that Alana didn't ask about Vince. "Yes, we're happy to be here."

"We have the executive suite for you, as you had requested, with a view of St. Patrick's. Is there anything else we can do for you?"

"No, thank you. We're good."

"Enjoy your stay, and please let us know if there is anything else we can do for you."

"Thank you."

The bellman took our luggage, and we got settled into our suite. Aunt Peg was drooling over the accommodations.

"My, Lord, you could cook Thanksgiving dinner in here," she said, as she walked into the kitchen of the suite. "And this table! My goodness, it's a shame to waste it. And look at this view! You can see the river. Which one is that?" she asked.

"The East River, Aunt Peg," I said.

"My, my. This is *Lifestyles of the Rich and Famous*," she said, as she and my mom went to their room. Emilie and Reese were already settled in and on their phones checking emails in the living room as they waited for us.

We quickly unpacked and were out the door of the hotel in no time. One of my favorite spots was Bergdorf's for lunch—not the fancy restaurant on the top floor, but the simple one on the lower level. We all enjoyed a glass of chardonnay and the tea sandwiches, as well as a cup of lobster bisque soup, my favorite. I felt relaxed, and it felt great to be in New York.

We had hair and nail appointments after lunch at Fekkai in Bendel's, so we walked down Fifth Avenue from Bergdorf's. We had to be at *The Colbert Report* by 5:00 p.m., and time was going quickly. As soon as we left the salon, we jumped into a cab over to the West Side and entered at the VIP entrance. There was a long line of people waiting in the general line. There was security inside, and shortly after we gave our names and told them we were guests of Amanda's, she appeared. Even though we had just seen her at Vince's funeral, she greeted us as if she had not seen us for a long time.

"Hey, guys, hello. How are you?" she said with a huge smile on her face. She was a beautiful girl and was dressed in jeans and a sweater. "So glad you could make it. Come with me. I'll take you upstairs and introduce you to the other writers."

We walked up a back staircase. The walls were filled with photographs of Stephen Colbert, as well as pictures of the writers with their Emmys. It was exciting to see Amanda in two of the pictures. Amanda appeared calm as she told us they were doing some rewrites for that night's show, but she had a few minutes to show us around.

Shortly thereafter, we got into the studio and a comedian did the warm up, followed by Stephen himself taking a few questions. He looked very handsome, and I was amazed how quickly he could come back with something funny to say after taking a question from an audience member who asked him whether he wore boxers or briefs. He quipped, "That's not personal enough. Next question?" It was great to laugh. When the show was over, Amanda was able to take us back stage to meet Stephen, and he couldn't have been nicer.

We asked Amanda to dinner, but she had another commitment. We had dinner reservations at Per Se at the Mandarin Oriental in the Time Warner Center where Vince and I had dined many times. Barbara Walters was at the table next to us, and my mom and Aunt Peg watched her every move.

"She hardly eats anything," said my mom.

It got to be comical, and I finally had to ask them to stop staring. Aunt Peg wanted to tell her that she liked "the view" from our table, playing off the name of her show, *The View*, but we wouldn't allow it. It ended up being a great day, and we were all pretty tired when we got back to the hotel.

The next day began with room service. It was much nicer to eat at our leisure in our suite than dressing first and going out to a restaurant. Emilie and Reese had gone for a run in the park and came back to the suite just as the attendant wheeled in a cart filled with fresh squeezed orange juice, croissants, berries, eggs, ham, and toast. It was beautifully presented with crystal glasses and shiny white plates, and we lounged in our sitting area, drinking coffee and stuffing ourselves.

"How was your run, girls?" I asked as they came in.

"Great, Mom," said Reese. "We saw Jennifer Aniston jogging."

"Who, dear?" asked Aunt Peg.

"From *Friends*, Aunt Peg, the television show."

"Oh, that's nice, dear."

I knew Aunt Peg had no idea who she was, but it didn't matter. I was glad the girls were able to get in some exercise. They took off their sneakers and had some breakfast.

"So, Mom, what's on the agenda for today?" asked Reese.

"Well," I said, putting down my coffee cup, "I thought we could do a museum and then some shopping. We have *La Boheme* tonight with dinner at Gilt before."

"Sounds good to me," said Reese.

I was beginning to think that maybe *La Boheme* wasn't the best choice. That emotional last scene between Rodolfo and Mimi was a real tearjerker, and I always cried when I saw it. "Okay, let's get a move on," I said, as we all got ready for another fun day.

"Maybe I'll find a dress for Samantha's wedding while we're here," said Emilie. I was happy to hear Emilie say something, since she had been so quiet. I was worried she wasn't having the best time.

"I should look for one for Caroline's wedding, too," said Reese.

The girls both found dresses, and we had a nice time at Gilt and the opera, despite all the emotion of the performance.

The morning of our last day began with a voicemail from Captain Martin asking me to call him. I'm ashamed to say that I didn't feel like ruining the respite from my life by returning the call, but I knew I had to. I made up an excuse that I needed something at the drug store and left the suite to call him.

"Martin," answered the voice at the other end of the line.

"Captain Martin, it's Clair."

"Yes, Mrs. Bondi, thank you for returning my call. We found Vince's phone."

My heart suddenly sank with the news, thinking that they might have listened to voicemail messages from Catherine and he was about to ask me who she was. I was afraid of what he was going to say next.

"Where did you find it?" I asked.

"Well, as you know, we've been combing the area ever since the shooting looking for clues, and we found it tossed in a wet, marshy area, so it's useless at this point."

"May I have the phone? I'd like to have it." I thought for sure he would want to keep it for evidence.

"Sure, it's all yours whenever you want it. It makes us think that the killer, or killers, really just wanted the money and his watch, so this fits with the whole premise that it was a robbery. They didn't care about the phone and just tossed it."

"Great work, Captain Martin," I said, relieved, almost too enthusiastically.

I walked back inside to the hotel. When I got to the suite, I overheard Emilie talking to Reese as I walked by their room.

"I'll be glad when this spectacle is over," said Emilie.

"Em, not too much longer. We only have to hang in a bit more."

I didn't say anything, but I felt really bad. They both hadn't wanted to come, after all. I should have gone into their room and apologized, but instead, I simply asked them if they wanted to leave a bit sooner than planned. They both agreed.

Emilie was going directly to her apartment since we were already in New York. She didn't have anything at home that she needed to have right away. Their lives, although changed, were going to go back to some sense of normalcy, with medical school and law school. My mom and Aunt Peg had a flight from Philly to Florida arranged for the next afternoon, so I would drive them to the airport. Reese's flight was also around the same time, so I could take everyone together. And I, unfortunately, would have to deal with a lot of things that couldn't be shared with anyone else.

Chapter 12

I soon realized after getting everyone to the airport that I had to get the house in Turks and Caicos ready for the new owners. The house was being sold furnished, so I didn't have to worry about that, but there were some clothes and personal items—mostly photographs—that I had to pack up. I could have had my cleaning service do it, but I wanted to stay in the house one last time. It was going to be really difficult to leave the house for good. I loved it so much.

As soon as I got home from the airport, I went online to see if there were any flights available for the next day. Since it wasn't high season, I wasn't sure if there would even be anything available. I thought that in the scheme of things, the short time away really wouldn't make much difference. I could still keep in touch with Captain Martin in case anything developed with the investigation, although as of the day before, nothing had changed—still no leads.

I was getting frustrated with the police work. How could they not find anyone who might know what had happened? Someone had to have either seen something at the time of the shooting or knew the person who did it. I had even put up a $50,000 reward for information regarding the shooter—yet still, nothing. The media coverage had lessened, for which I was grateful. There were no longer any reporters outside my home, so the police coverage was gone, too.

The 7:00 a.m. flight was booked, but there was another flight at 2:30 p.m. I booked a seat and kept the return open in case I had to come back sooner than the two weeks. After phoning Charles and arranging for an 11:00 a.m. pick up, I decided to call Barb. I hadn't even talked to her about what had happened leading up to Vince's death. I hadn't told her about my having Vince followed or about Catherine. I knew she was going to be shocked, to say the least. She had called a few times when I was in New York, but it wasn't the right time to talk. I had so much to tell, and I certainly wasn't about to talk in front of the girls or my mom and aunt. Barb would be the only person who would know all I was going to tell, with the exception of Chris.

I was able to reach Barb, but I was surprised by her reaction. She felt something had been going on all along. "Clair, come on, you told me he was with her a lot, on both coasts. Was that really necessary? I'm so sorry that this all came about, or I should say, was discovered now that Vince is dead. It really doesn't matter."

"Doesn't matter?" I asked. "Are you kidding? It matters greatly."

"I mean, what are you going to do with the information? It's not like Vince is still alive, and you decided to get a divorce. I'm sure you aren't going to tell anyone. Or are you? Are you going to tell the girls?"

"Heavens, no. I mean, no, I'm not telling anyone, especially the girls. Two affairs were two too many to stay married. But I want the girls to remember their father without that information. They've been through enough already."

"And what about what you have been through? I worry about you."

She, too, like Chris, thought I had been wasting my time with Vince. She never bought his stories about why he didn't want to be with me sexually. It's crazy how something can just click and then you see it, when it was there right in front of you the entire time. Maybe it's true what the therapists say: sometimes we just don't want to see something that's too painful. I don't think, however, that was true in my case. I just couldn't believe he would cheat on me again. It was as simple as that.

I slept in the next morning, which felt great. I hadn't been able to do that for weeks. I left for the airport at one o'clock after packing a small bag to hold a jacket and some magazines to read on the plane. I had makeup there at the house, so I didn't have to bring any of that with me. Charles was right on time, as always.

I was usually over-the-top excited when I went to Turks, but this time was different. I wasn't excited, but sad. I hadn't even told the girls or my mom that I was going. I didn't want to bother them since they had all just gotten back in place themselves. I would tell them after I was there a day or so.

I couldn't stop thinking about the girls. I wished now they were near one another, rather than being such a long distance apart. I knew they could always call or email, but it wasn't the same as being able to see one another in person. I planned on talking to them about some therapy with a professional for a few months or however long they needed it. It was the least I could do.

There wasn't any rush-hour traffic at noon, so I didn't have to allow for more than the expected twenty minutes to get to the airport. The flight was direct, so in just about three hours we were on the ground in Providenciales. Of everywhere I had been in the world, I loved Turks the most. I loved the island, the people, the gorgeous blue water, and most especially, my house. There was no place that brought me such joy.

I couldn't help but reminisce about my first walk on the beach from our hotel on Grace Bay ten years ago when I saw the most beautiful house I had ever seen. It was magical, with mahogany-colored French doors that opened to the outside, almost calling the voyager to come and take a look. Its thatched roof, white masonry siding, and island-blue trim made it so appealing. It was surreal how the bougainvillea draped around the house, its vivid red in stark contrast to the white and blue. But the thing that drew me to the place was the gazebo with its black iron light fixture. It made me want the house more than anything I had ever wanted in my life. I imagined myself sitting outside and looking at the beautiful sea.

There was something about houses that had a visceral effect on me. I think it began back when I was an early teen and watched the television show *Family*. I loved how the show began, with the mom in her beautiful living room with a black baby grand piano topped with gorgeous silver-framed photographs of the family looking so happy.

I remember how excited I was to tell Vince that I had found a place for us to live. All we needed to do was find out who owned it and tell the person we wanted to buy it. It didn't matter that it wasn't up for sale. I knew that we could buy it if we made the owners a deal they couldn't resist. That's what I wanted to do. All I had to do was convince Vince.

It didn't take much convincing to get Vince to agree to buy the house. Vince loved beautiful homes, too. He liked a certain lifestyle—a lifestyle that would spotlight his success, and this house fit that perfectly.

We contacted the top broker in Provo, and he talked to the

owners. They took our offer, and the house became ours. I tore it apart and made it the house of my dreams. I named it Blakely House. Blake was my father's middle name, and I always loved it. If I had had a son, that would have been his name. I suppose I could have named one of the girls Blake, but I didn't think of it back then. So Blakely House it was, and it was paradise. Everyone on the island knew of the house, so we quickly became a prominent name around the island. We socialized with the top builders, bankers, and well-to-do people from around the world who came to Turks and had a residence there.

I breezed through customs and immigration and in no time was in a cab en route to my house. There was always a slew of cabs waiting outside the airport, so I never arranged for transportation. Vince kept a Range Rover at the house, which I always thought was a bit extravagant, but there was no need to have someone drive it to pick me up. We threw the car in with the price of the house to the new owners, and it got the house sold more quickly. We didn't make anything on the car, or so Vince had said, but with all the revelations as of late about money and the state of our real estate holdings, I wasn't sure of anything anymore. This visit was certainly bittersweet.

It was about six thirty when I got to the house, my favorite time of night. I unlocked the door, walked over to the French doors, and opened them up. The view was breathtaking—the blue-orange sky atop the blue water at sunset. I walked outside and looked to the left, where the beach turned and the sun was setting. I kicked off my shoes and walked to the water's edge, holding my skirt up with my hands. The thought of having to give this up tore at my heart. The saddest part of thinking about the house was that we rarely made love there in the last few years. To have been in the most romantic place on the face of the earth and not to have shared it intimately was such a waste.

All of a sudden, I heard, "Hello." I looked back at the house, and there was an attractive man, about mid-fifties with a great head of black hair, walking toward me with a big smile on his face.

"Yes?" I said, interested to find out who the person was. I didn't recognize him.

"Mrs. Bondi," he said, with a charming British accent, "I'm Leon Abramson, First Caribbean Bank. I hope I'm not getting you at a bad time."

"Oh, no, not at all," I said. "How can I help you?"

"Alex Sloane told me you were arriving today." Alex was the agent who had sold us the house and was handling the sale to the new buyers.

"Oh, yes," I said. "I just got here." We were standing on the terrace, so I moved my hand to the seat of the chair, suggesting that he sit down.

"Mrs. Bondi . . ."

"Please call me Clair."

"Okay, of course, Clair. I wanted to come by to express my condolences about Vince's death."

"Thank you," I said. "That's really kind of you." I was a bit confused. I couldn't imagine why Leon would be coming to see me. I didn't even know him. "I remember we had used your bank when we first bought the house ten years ago, but that's really all that I know. Did you know Vince?"

"I always dealt with Vince, but I assure you that I will take very good care of your account from here on in."

"Account?" I asked.

"Your account. Well, yours and Vince's, although all the money was deposited in your name."

"Mr. Abramson . . ."

"Please call me Leon."

"Leon, what account are you speaking of?"

"Your $8 million account."

"What $8 million account?" I asked in disbelief.

"You aren't aware?" he said, opening his eyes wide and raising his eyebrows. "There's been a million dollars a year deposited into a joint account with a check from you for the last eight years. And you didn't know about it?"

I tried to compose myself, but I felt like I was beginning to get lightheaded. "No, I did not."

"Well then, you and I need to talk. I really don't know what to say other than you have a lot of money in an account that you obviously didn't know about. Why don't you come over to the bank tomorrow, and I will show you everything? Now might not be the best time to discuss with you just getting here and all."

"Leon, this house is going to be sold to its new owners in two weeks. Is there any way possible to prevent the sale? I want to keep it."

"Well, interesting you should say that. I understand the new buyers haven't been able to sell their home in Grand Cayman, so they might want to back out. I'll check on that for you first thing tomorrow morning. Can you come over at eleven?"

"Yes. I will be there."

"Okay. I'm sorry you didn't know about all of this, but I assure you the money is yours. We'll talk tomorrow."

"Yes, we will." *We certainly will.*

Chapter 13

Eight million dollars, and Vince never told me about it. Unbelievable. *Why?* I couldn't stop asking myself that same question, over and over again. It wasn't like he just had it in his name. It was in both our names. That made me believe he didn't really want to hide it from me but, instead, wanted to have it where it was available to me. Only he didn't want me to know about it, for some unexplained reason. It kept me up all night thinking about it. Was it for tax reasons that he did it? My accountant and lawyer never mentioned the money when I met with them. Did they know about it? Should I ask them about it? I was so confused.

I got up and walked over to the French doors facing the ocean. It was dark—really dark. I could barely see the white caps of the waves as they hit the shore. I cracked the door; I could hear the sound of the waves gently hitting the sand, but I couldn't see the water or the moon. The sky was dark; there were no stars out. Usually in Turks the bright North Star is visible, but tonight it was nowhere to be seen. I wanted to go outside down to the water, but I didn't think that was a good thing to do. I quickly closed the doors and locked them.

I stood for a moment with my back against the doors and my hands behind my back holding onto the doorknobs. The house felt eerie, sort of like the Villanova house when I went there after I found out about Vince's affair from the detective. I didn't like that feeling. Everything felt like it was closing in on me. I wanted it to be morning. It was three o'clock. What was I going to do till morning?

Thank God Leon came to express his condolences, or I wouldn't have known about the money. I felt relieved that there was a chance that I could possibly keep the house. I would still be able to have the girls down and enjoy gorgeous Turks and Caicos— jumping in the surf, lying out by the pool, playing tennis, and taking long walks on the beach—all the things I enjoyed so much.

I tried to just think about those fun things to come, but my mind kept going to the darker place where I felt like I was drowning in all of this mess, as if Vince's death wasn't enough. I hadn't even told the girls or my mom that I had gone to Turks and Caicos. What if there were an emergency? They wouldn't even know where I was. I was starting to panic, frozen with fear. I fell onto the bed. There was a picture of Vince fishing with Emilie on the end table. They looked so happy. *Oh, God, please let me get through the night. Please, Lord, please.*

I don't remember falling asleep, but I found myself in bed with the sun up and shining into the room. I could see flakes of dust in the air where the sun gleamed in, making them feel like fairy dust. I was turned sideways in the bed. I straightened my body out and centered myself, propping myself up a bit. The room looked beautiful. Everything in the room was white: the beamed ceiling, the walls, the rug, the bed, the linens, and the furniture. There were silver-framed prints of white hydrangeas over the bed, and the lamps were white, too. The sun danced upon the room, and it felt so different from the earlier unsettling darkness of night.

It always amazed me how morning brought the hope of a new day. No matter what seemed daunting the night before seemed better in the morning light.

I decided I had to let my mom and the girls know where I was. I reached for my iPad and sent them a message: "Had to go to Turks to get house ready for new owners, but decided to keep!" I tried to sound upbeat so that they wouldn't worry, and I didn't get into why I was keeping the house. I would explain later that I couldn't part with it.

Neither my mom nor the girls had any idea there were money issues, so I felt comfortable that they wouldn't question my decision to keep it. They knew I hadn't been happy with Vince's decision to want to sell it, so they would figure now that Vince was no longer here, I decided to keep it for our family. I knew they would be happy about the decision since everyone loved being there.

I grabbed my robe and walked outside. There was always a gentle breeze, and I could feel the air whip underneath my robe onto my body.

I held out the bottom with my hands on each side, allowing the air to flow more freely. I felt for an instant like Francesca in the movie *Bridges of Madison County* when she walked onto her porch in the evening and did the same thing. I never tired of the view. I sat down on the rock wall and dangled my feet over the side. They didn't reach the sand, but almost. Everywhere I looked there was beauty.

A few birds flew overhead, and I could see a boat in the distance. I thought about the people on that boat. Were they nestled body to body as they had slept the night away with the rhythm of the sea? I was jealous, and I didn't even know the people. I told myself to concentrate on the matter at hand: figuring out the reason for the money in the secret account.

Then I thought of Leon. He seemed like a really nice man. I wondered what his story was. I didn't know anything about him other than he was the chairman of the bank. I wondered if he were married. I would think, yes—he seemed the married type, like he had a beautiful wife who loved him. I wondered if they enjoyed living in Turks. How could they not?

It was still very early in the morning, and I didn't have to meet him until eleven. I decided to put on my swimsuit and take a walk along the beach and perhaps a dip in the ocean.

I walked down the beach by all the new condos. Development was everywhere in Provo. One after another, luxurious buildings were going up and sales were brisk, bringing people to the island from all over the world. There were a few people walking, mostly couples. I tried to calm myself down and convince myself that things would fall into place. I would eventually find out the answers to a lot of questions. I had to believe that. The police would find out who killed Vince, and I would find out why Vince didn't tell me about the money. Surely he was looking out for me by having the money in a joint account, and I was sure that he never thought he would die before my finding out about it. There had to be an explanation. There just had to be.

I didn't walk too far, but instead, came back to the house and went into the ocean. I could feel the stress leaving my body with each step I took. The gorgeous salted-blue water traveled up my body and took with it the pain of the past week. How could two weeks make such a difference in one's life? Now, Vince was gone, and each day I had to deal with the investigation, the sorrow, and a broken heart, plus all the financial issues. To have heard from my accountant and lawyer that things weren't as I had thought they were financially, and now to hear from Leon that there really was money—well, I didn't know what to think. The bottom line was Vince lied to me, or I should say, kept information from me—important information, like the $8 million. What if I had never found out about it? I couldn't stop thinking about it, and the more I thought about it, the more it made me angry.

I showered and put on a white knit straight skirt with a navy blue sleeveless top and tan heels. I blew out my hair and put on some makeup, which felt good. I drove to the bank in my black Range Rover, or I should say, Vince's Range Rover. We were the only people on the island part-time who drove one. We were easily spotted when driving about, and that's the reason Vince wanted it. He loved the recognition. He loved it when someone wanted to know who he was.

I walked through the glass doors with etched white letters saying *First Caribbean Bank* and could see Leon in his office through the reception area. He happened to look up from his desk and noticed me. He smiled, got up, and walked toward me. He had on a navy-blue sports jacket with a blue checked shirt, no tie, tan gabardine trousers, and a pair of black Gucci loafers. His dark hair was slightly curled at his neck.

"Hello, Clair," he said, as he reached out his hand. "How are you today?"

"Good, Leon." I surely wasn't good.

"Come in. Can I get you anything? Coffee, tea?" His secretary stood nearby, ready to supply whatever I wanted.

"No, thanks."

With that, she left the room and closed the door, giving Leon a nod of her head.

"Please, have a seat," he said, as he pulled the chair out for me to a small round table in the corner of his office. He took a seat and grabbed a folder from his desk, which was marked *Bondi,*

Vincent and Clair, Blakely House, Providenciales, T&C. It felt strange to see our names written together, and it hit me that I would never write our names that way again.

"Clair, I have been thinking a lot about you and your situation of having to deal with such a horrific chain of events. First, just let me say I am truly sorry."

"Thank you, Leon. I appreciate that. Just trying to take one day at a time."

"Well, I would think that is the best attitude to have." At that, he opened the file and took out a form that I could see had both Vince's and my signatures, although my signature did not look the same as how I signed my name.

"Here is the form that was set up eight years ago with both your signatures, but yours was signed by Vince with his right as power of attorney for you. So assuming you didn't know about the money, I would also assume you weren't aware that Vince had signed this for you? Is that correct?"

"Yes, that is correct. I knew that he had power of attorney. There were so many times that he would need my signature, and it was just easier if he could sign for me."

"I understand," said Leon. "The good news is that you were aware of this type of arrangement, so it isn't like you were blindsided about Vince signing things for you."

"But that still doesn't explain why he never told me about this. It's just so strange. If he didn't want me to know about this money, why wouldn't he have just set up the account in his name? Why would he bother to put it in both of our names?"

"Clair, we have many clients who place money in our banking system here in the Turks and Caicos to better handle their tax situations. As you are probably aware, money kept here is not reported back to the United States regarding your income tax filings. Possibly, your husband used both of your names because that was how you did everything else financially—jointly."

"I think you could be right, Leon. That is the only reason it could be. Vince never thought he was going to die before he told me about it."

"That very well could be. So now, going forward, I would suggest that you keep the money here so you can continue to proceed in the same manner. If you take the money out and bring it back to an account in the United States, you will have to pay taxes on it."

"Yes, I understand. There are still a lot of things up in the air right now for me financially, so I will have to see about all of this. I see no reason for bringing this to the attention of my accountant and lawyer. It could cause some problems, and that is the last thing I want to do. I guess I will just keep it here."

Just then, my eyes glanced over to the credenza behind his desk. There was a framed photo of Leon with a woman and a boy, around ten years old, standing in front of a regal-looking building.

"Leon, is that a photo of your family?" I knew I must have seemed distracted and that Leon might have thought it was odd for me to mention. I wasn't sure it was his family because he looked a lot younger than he did now.

"Yes, it is, or it was. Well, I should explain. Clair, my wife and son were killed in a car accident ten years ago when we lived in London. Jan was picking Ethan up from school and a drunk driver plowed into them. Ethan was in the fifth grade."

"Oh, my God, Leon. I'm so sorry," I said, thinking how horrible it must have been for him to lose both his wife and son.

"Thank you. I moved here to Turks and Caicos because I felt I couldn't stay there with the memory of losing my family. Since the island is British owned, it worked with coming here to continue my work in banking."

"I can certainly understand," I said, as my eye caught another photo of Leon, which I could see was more recent. In that one he was standing in the middle of a group of dark-skinned children, all with huge smiles on their faces. "And what about the other photo—the one with the group of children? What is the story there?"

"That's the Haitian earthquake from 2010. I helped out a bit. We're only about eighty miles away, so a group of us did some reconstruction work there, helping to build back the island. It's still a mess and we continue to help out, but it's going to take a long time and a lot of money."

Is this guy for real? He loses his wife and son and comes here and now is helping out people from an earthquake? "You are an amazing man, Leon." I thought when I said it that maybe I was getting too personal, but I was very moved by what had happened to him and what he was doing for others.

"Well, it isn't just me, as I have mentioned. Lots of people have helped." He then changed the subject back to the money and said as he stood up, "So Clair, do you have any other questions for me, or can I be of assistance in any other way? I know it has got to be quite a shock."

I was shocked all right, but even more shocked by what came out of my mouth next. "Yes, I do have a question. Would you like to come over for dinner tonight? I need a break from all of this, and one way that I can relax is by cooking." I stood up and held my breath waiting for his answer, but he answered right away with certainty.

"Sure. Love to, that is, if you're sure you want to go through all that trouble."

"No trouble at all. I'll pick up some steaks at the IGA, and we can grill. Real simple."

"Okay, then. You're on."

"Seven good?"

"Seven's great." With that, he walked me to the door and held it open as I walked past him.

Chapter 14

As I got into my car, I couldn't believe what had just happened. I had invited a man I hardly knew to dinner after my husband had just been fatally shot a few weeks ago. How did that happen? It was so out of character for me, but it just came out. And, I was even more shocked that Leon had agreed to come.

For the first time in several weeks, I felt excited about something in the storm of a lot of heartache. It was something different to focus on, but truthfully, the most surprising thing was that I was attracted to Leon. After all the years of being with Vince, I never imagined that I would be thinking about another man. It was something that was not expected.

As I watched and listened to Leon talk, I enjoyed the soothing sound of his voice, sort of like Tom Brokaw's, only with a British accent—a voice that exuded strength, kindness, and, at the same time, sex appeal. I hoped that he hadn't found my invitation too rash or inappropriate, but he had accepted. I decided I needed to stop thinking about it and focus on what I was going to make him—us—for dinner.

I drove up Lee Highway to the IGA and got all the food I needed. Miss Winnie's Pies was adjacent to the grocery store, so I was able to pick that up without making another stop. I wanted to be done with all the shopping so I could spend the afternoon getting a massage at the Regent Palms. The spa there was so gorgeous, and I got one regularly when I was "on island," as the natives say, from Amor, an incredible woman who gave a great deep tissue massage. I called her from my car, and luckily, she was free.

I put all the food away and got back into the car to go for the massage. When I pulled up, I saw several people from the hotel that I knew. They treated me normally, with a smile and a hello, so I figured they didn't know about Vince's death. For a moment, it felt good not to have to explain everything like I had to do at home.

When I got to the locker room and changed out of my clothes into my robe, I realized that I had lost a considerable amount of weight. I hadn't noticed it until then, but when I tied the belt to the robe, I felt my waist was much smaller. I decided to weigh myself, and sure enough, I had lost ten pounds. I was normally 125, but now I was 115. I looked more like I did ten years ago—my breasts appeared perkier and my stomach was flatter. It wasn't a time to be thinking about weight, but at the same time, I felt good about it.

I walked out into the waiting area, and Amor greeted me. "Miss Clair," she said, smiling, "it is so wonderful to see you. How have you been?"

I tried to fight back the tears, but I couldn't.

"Miss Clair, what is wrong?" she said, putting her arms around me.

"Amor, I have terrible news. My husband died. He was shot in a robbery."

"Oh, I am so sorry, Miss Clair." Her large brown eyes couldn't contain her tears, and we both wept and hugged. After we composed ourselves, we spent some time talking, and she spent more time than normal working my body over. I left the spa feeling better physically and actually more in touch with my body than ever. With Vince's holding back of sex, I didn't have a positive body image. A woman can lose a sense of her physical self when she isn't touched. And, oh, how I craved it.

I got home and started getting things ready for dinner. I put on some Lionel Richie, and the house felt alive. The French doors were open to the beach, and the gentle breeze came through the house. It was four o'clock by then, and I started to think about what I was going to wear when Leon came. I went to my closet and looked through an array of sundresses, which were always great to wear on the island. I tried a couple on, but with the weight loss, some of them hung on me. But then I remembered a black Lycra shift that had previously been a bit tight. I put it on, and it fit great. It was sleeveless and very simple, but it was perfect. I put a pair of silver wedged sandals with it and knew it was the right choice. With that decided, I poured a glass of Chardonnay and sat outside on a lounge chair and just stared at the sea. The constant breeze felt so nice and, for the first time in weeks, I actually felt okay.

My phone beeped, and there was a text from Leon. "Clair, are you sure I can't bring something tonight? Leon." I wrote back, "No, I have everything under control. Thanks, anyhow." I could tell Leon was a good man. I could just feel it.

And then came a call from Detective Martin. When I saw on the caller ID that it was a call from him, I took a deep breath and answered. "Detective Martin, hello," I said. "How are you?"

"Hello, Clair. Good, good. I'm good." He seemed like he

had something important to say and wanted to get right to the purpose of his call. "Clair, I am happy to say that we are close to making an arrest. We feel we have our man, or I should say, our kid."

"Oh my gosh," I blurted out. "Who is it?"

"A kid from the neighborhood who has already served some time as an accomplice to another murder. He's only twenty-three, but he's been cleared as having been in that area at the time. I can't really say anymore at this time, but I think it won't be too long until we have him in custody. We want to follow him for a bit longer and then close in on him. We have some kids in the hood who gave us the lead."

"Wow. Hard to believe that someone of his age could do such a thing," was all I could say.

"Well, sadly, it happens a lot. I just wanted to let you know. Let's keep this between you and me for right now until we definitely see how things pan out, but we're pretty sure."

"Okay. Thank you, Detective Martin."

"Sure. Stay safe. Call me if you need anything."

I hung up the phone and debated whether to call the girls and tell them, but then I thought it best to follow Detective Martin's request to keep it quiet. I sat and looked out to the sea. A group of birds were flying over the water, dipping down to the surf and then up to the sand. I watched as they clustered together, staying all in a group. I missed my group—Vince and the girls and me. I decided to put it aside, and I did feel some relief, thinking that maybe all of this could be over and we could all go about living our lives in a "new normal." For the next two weeks I wanted to stay in Turks and just relax and then return and figure things out with my accountant and the secret money, as well as the investigation. I desperately needed a break.

Time passed by quickly, and before I knew it, it was six

thirty. I changed into the dress I had laid out and freshened up my makeup. I had my hair up and then down, and then up again. I decided to stop fooling with it and just put it in a knot at the back of my neck.

As I was walking from my bedroom into the living room, I saw Leon standing at the front door. He rang the doorbell, and I opened the door. He looked so handsome and had a bouquet of flowers.

"Hi," I said, with a smile.

"Hello," he said, holding out the flowers. "This was the least I could do. I hope you like hydrangeas."

How did he know? I suppose he didn't, but maybe he liked them, too.

Leon had on a powder-blue shirt and jeans and a pair of brown Gucci loafers. I loved a man who dressed well, and Leon certainly did. He was right out of *GQ*.

"Oh, my," I said, perhaps too gushy, "I love hydrangeas. Come in, please."

He came in, and I quickly went into the kitchen to get a vase and water.

"Make yourself at home," I said, as I tended to the flowers. "Pour yourself a drink from the bar. There's some champagne chilling, if you would like to start with that."

"Is that what you would like?" he asked.

"Sure," I said. "Champagne is always a good way to start." I was known for always starting with a glass of champagne when I entertained. It felt the most festive—the glass, the bubbles, the taste. I had a small bottle chilling, enough for two glasses.

"This is some house," he said, turning around in a circle, taking the place in. "I've never been in here before. I'm really glad you were able to keep it. A place this gorgeous would be tough to give up."

"You are so right about that, and I owe that all to you. I'll give you a tour if you like."

"Clair," he said, rather cautiously, "I just want to say again how sorry I am for the loss of your husband."

"Thank you, Leon. I appreciate that."

There was a moment of silence that felt rather awkward. I wasn't sure if he was happy to be at my house under the circumstances. He looked unsure of himself, like maybe he shouldn't have been there with me.

"Leon," I said, "I can't change what has happened. I have to now move forward with my life as a widow. I never thought I would find myself in this situation, but I am. I'm sure you never thought you would have lost your wife and son, so you know what it feels like."

"Unfortunately, yes, I do. And you are spot on with your assessment of the situation."

"Please, let's go outside and sit down," I said, as I started out the door.

Leon followed with the two champagne flutes and said, "Yes, it would be a shame to ignore that gorgeous view."

He let me walk through the doorway and stood by the door as I walked by him. We sat across from one another as the sun set. I had put out some olives and cheese beforehand, so we nibbled on that. I took my champagne glass and said, "To Turks. The best place in the world."

"Do you really mean that, Clair, that Turks is the best place in the world?" he asked.

"Oh, yes," I said, as I put my glass down after taking a sip of the champagne. "No place like it."

"Have you traveled a great deal?" he asked, putting down his glass.

"Yes, fortunately. Vince and I were big fans of Italy and France.

I should say, it was I more than Vince who loved France, but he went along. I'm grateful that I had those experiences."

"For sure," he said.

"Did you and your wife travel much?" I asked.

"Actually, no. Well, I did for business, but Jan was more of a homebody, so I would try to stay a little longer when I went somewhere to do a little sightseeing."

All I could think of was how sad that was—this wonderful, kind, handsome man traveling around by himself because his wife wouldn't go with him. "Wow." I decided to change the subject. "So, tell me about you, Leon. What is it like living here? Living here in paradise, I should say."

"It certainly is," he said. "I love the water, so I'm in my boat a lot when I'm not working."

"What kind of boat do you have?" I asked.

"I've got a sailboat."

"Sounds really nice. Where do you dock?"

"Right up from here in Leeward."

I loved the water, so all of this was sounding very appealing. "And you can handle that yourself?"

"Sometimes," he said, with a grin.

"How wonderful." I couldn't help but envision him working the sails in his gorgeous sailboat with the wind at his back and the sun setting on the water.

"Clair," he said, as he leaned forward and looked at me, "it's really a pleasure to be here with you." I started to interrupt him, not accepting the compliment, and then he said, "Clair, seriously, I have heard so many great things about you—how nice you are and your work with designing and building houses back in the States."

"Well, thank you. I love what I do, and I love being here, so we both have things that mean a lot to us, which is a good thing."

I raised my glass and made a toast: "Here's to enjoying what we love." And, on that note, I said, "I'll be right back with the steaks."

"Let me cook those for you."

"I was hoping you would say that. The grill is right over there," I said, as I nodded my head to the right, "and it's already lit."

"Terrific."

As I walked through the house to the kitchen, I could hardly contain my excitement. Leon was fabulous, and I loved having him here. He was interesting, and I was attracted to him. I was into the whole boat thing. I could picture myself on it, lounging on the deck as he worked the sails.

Dinner turned out great with Leon mastering the steaks. You really can't go wrong with steak, baked potatoes, and salad, not to mention a great bottle of Cabernet. We sat and talked for several hours about a myriad of subjects—from real estate to politics. The night grew chilly, and I went inside and got a wrap. I had a fire pit, which we lit, so it was very nice to be sitting outside. The sound of the gentle breaking of the waves set the tone for complete relaxation. As the night progressed and we shared personal information, Leon told me about his wife.

"Jan was a personal trainer but was bipolar, so she had trouble keeping clients because she didn't always show up. I would come home and never know what I was going to step into. Some days she was good, but others she just would close up and spend time by herself."

"That must have been awfully difficult to deal with."

"Yes, it was. I felt sorry for her, and I tried everything to get her help, but there was only so much that could be done."

"How did you get involved in 2010 with that devastating earthquake in Haiti?" I asked, changing the subject.

"Well, since we're so close physically, just ninety miles away, and the fact that so many people from there work here, in Turks,

I wanted to help. And, I had the time and resources to do it, so it was good for me."

To say I was impressed with Leon was an understatement. This man had turned his life around after his own tragedy and spent his time since then helping others.

It was almost midnight, and we had finished the night with coffee and Miss Winnie's pie, which was a big hit. He helped me bring the dishes to the kitchen, and as I walked him to the door, he turned to me and said, "Clair, might you want to go sailing tomorrow night around sunset? That is, if you are free and feel up to it?" *This was surreal. This terrific man was going to take me out on his boat, at sunset no less.*

"What can I bring?" I asked, rather than answering the question directly.

"Just you."

Chapter 15

After a run on the beach the next morning with thoughts of Leon and our sunset sail later on, I thought I had better call Alex Sloane, the agent who had put Blakely House under contract. I wanted to let him know how much I appreciated his help, through Leon, to cancel the sale.

After being connected through his receptionist at Turks and Caicos Realty, I was able to reach him. He greeted me with kindness when he picked up the phone.

"Clair, hello. How are you? So nice to hear from you."

"Hello, Alex. My apology for not getting to you sooner."

"Clair, no problem. Leon explained to me that you decided not to sell, and I can't blame you. I'm excited for you to keep your beautiful home."

"You're right about that, Alex. I do love it." I could feel myself smiling.

"And Clair, my deepest, deepest condolences over Vince. I was so shocked to hear, and I hope that your family will be a great source of strength to you in the coming days."

"Thank you." I wanted to ask him some things about Leon but wasn't sure how to go about it without sounding too forward. "Everyone has been so nice, and it was especially thoughtful of Leon to stop by and talk a bit."

"Oh, Leon. He's one of a kind, that's for sure. Great guy."

I also didn't want to act like I didn't know that we had an account at his bank, let alone $8 million in it, so I simply said, "Banks in the States don't give their customers such personal attention."

"Yes, and that's why I had suggested using him when you and Vince first came here. He certainly stands out from everyone else. Ownership makes all the difference."

"Ownership?" I asked, trying to play down my surprise.

"Leon owns the First Caribbean bank here in Turks. He decided to live here because he loves it, just like you and I do. Lucky for us and lucky for me because any client I have ever referred to him loves him, too."

"I didn't know that," I said. Leon was so nice and down-to-earth that I never would have thought he had that level of wealth and position.

"Clair, please let me know if there's anything I can do for you, both now or in the future. Do you think you'll be spending more time here now?" he asked.

"I hope so, Alex. I would like that very much."

"Great. Make sure you keep in touch."

"Yes, most certainly. Thank you."

I left the bed unmade and my half-eaten yogurt container in the sink and spent the afternoon lying by the pool. It was amazing what the sun did to make me feel better, not to mention the added boost to my highlights. As I lay in the sun, I felt an unexpected attraction to someone other than Vince. One thing was for sure: I liked thinking about Leon, and with each new bit of information, that attraction grew stronger.

Leon sent a text that he would pick me up at four thirty and wrote, "Great day for a sunset." I was getting excited, but at the same time, I had the stress of figuring out what to wear. Of course, I had to have on a bathing suit, but which one—a bikini or a one piece, a sundress over it or boy shorts with a top? I wanted to look good—and sexy—but I didn't want to appear too seductive. At the same time, I didn't want to look too buttoned up. I wanted to look relaxed, but I knew I wasn't going to be, or at least I didn't think I could be, because frankly, I was nervous.

After trying on several bathing suits, the white bikini looked best with white boy shorts and a black tank top. I loved how the tie of the bikini top showed at the neck when a top was placed over it. A pair of camel-colored platform sandals won out. I figured they would be good for climbing onto the boat, and I could take them off once on board.

The afternoon passed quickly, so I headed to the shower and took a glass of chardonnay with me, hoping it would make me feel more relaxed. The sun was streaming in through the glass skylight as I washed my hair. The shower gel glided over my body as I cupped it in my hand. My tan lines were more prominent after the day's sun.

I blew out my hair, pulled it back in a knot at my neck, and put on a little makeup—just some tinted moisturizer, lipstick, and waterproof mascara. I skipped the sunscreen, although I knew I shouldn't, but I always felt so greasy with it on. After all, it wasn't the height of the afternoon sun, or at least that's how I rationalized not applying it. I wanted to have a second glass of wine but thought it best to pass. I put on my bikini, the top and shorts, and packed a long-sleeve shirt in my small backpack.

And then, there was the slight knock on the doorframe of the

French doors, even though they were open.

"Hey, how are you?" I heard, as I turned to the door. The sight of Leon standing there with the backdrop of the sand and blue sea made my heart leap. He had on yellow swim shorts, a white golf shirt, and boat shoes. He also had a huge smile on his face and looked very relaxed.

"Great," I replied, as I grabbed my bag.

"Let me get that," he said, as he took it from my hand. His shoulder brushed mine, and I looked up at him. "All set?" he asked. His brown eyes were piercing against his tanned face and dark hair.

"Yes, let's go. I'm excited to see your boat."

"Well, it's waiting for us. Beautiful evening." He closed the door behind us, and we walked to his black Porsche. It was the same one as Vince's. He opened the door for me, and we drove off with the top down. Riding along Lee Highway up to Leeward, I could see the ocean between the condos and the newly developed retail spaces as we made our way out to the marina. It was only a short drive, so we were there in about fifteen minutes.

We drove into the parking lot, but then drove down a narrow path that didn't really look like a road or entrance to anywhere. I wasn't sure where we were going, but about a quarter mile down the way was a sailboat in the distance, standing by itself. There were no other boats around it, and I almost died when I saw it. It was the most beautiful yacht I had ever seen—huge, brown mahogany with glorious white sails. As we drove closer, I was able to see the name of Leon's boat: *London Bridge*. Two men were leaving the dock and getting into their car when we passed them. They gave Leon a wave. He gave them one back.

"Wow," I said. "You said we were going on your sailboat, not a yacht. This is amazing!"

"I hope you'll like it," he said as he pulled up and got out of the car.

We walked onto the dock, which was quite long, and he helped me on board, taking my hand. He started the engine and took command of the large, teak wheel. We started out of the harbor, the sun cascading upon the deck. The yacht had to be nearly fifty feet long, and it had white leather seating, both chairs and banquettes, with lots of pillows in blue and yellow stripe.

"Get comfortable," he said. "I just need to get us out a bit, and then we can anchor. I thought we'd go along the shore line, if that's okay with you."

God, Almighty. Anything he wants to do is more than fine with me. "Sure," I said. "Gorgeous."

He was checking some things with the controls. It was obvious he knew just what he was doing. I was beginning to relax. I sat down on one of the banquettes and put my face up toward the sun.

He glanced over and said, smiling, "Seems like you enjoy the sun. So do I."

I smiled back and asked, "So how long is this yacht?"

"Forty-two feet."

"Is the decking all teak?"

"Yes."

"Wow. Really beautiful," I said, as I reached down and moved my hand over the floor.

"I'll be able to stop shortly, and we can just relax and talk a bit, or take a swim if you like."

"Sounds great."

There was no one around. We were the only boaters in the area, and all we could see was the sand and the beautiful blue water. After about fifteen minutes, we stopped and Leon did a few things with the sails and shut off the motor.

"There we go. We can settle here a bit. Let me get you

something to drink." He started downstairs.

"Can I help?" I asked.

"Sure. Come on down."

I followed him.

"Watch your step."

When I got to the lower level, there was a kitchen with a built-in table, a sitting area, and a few closed doors, which I assumed were to the bedrooms and head. The kitchen had a full Sub-Zero refrigerator, which Leon opened. He took out a bottle of Veuve Clicquot.

"Oh, nice," I said, smiling, thinking this guy really knew me. How special that he remembered that I liked champagne, especially Veuve. He brought out a plate of cheese and fruit, and we went back up to the deck. We sat together on the banquette and put the drink and food on the table in front of us.

"So how did this all happen?" I asked. "This yacht, your life here." I picked up a strawberry and bit into it.

"Well, as you know from the other night, I, too, had to put my life back together after my loss, so I decided to do that here in Turks. I used to live in Chelsea, which I loved, back in London, but I needed a change. Too many reminders of where I was. I felt smothered."

"I can understand that," I said.

"I got involved with my work, my charity work, etc. It's been good."

"What about the rest of your family? Siblings, parents?"

"I'm an only child and was adopted, so my adoptive parents are in South Africa, as well as my birth mother."

"Wow. That's really interesting." I couldn't imagine what else I was going to discover about Leon.

"I went to college in London and just stayed there. I met Jan there, as well. We married right out of college."

"Ah, young love," I said, smiling. "Me, too. I met Vince in college and married young."

"Do you regret that?" he asked, taking a sip of his champagne.

"Well, yes and no. I'm glad I had the girls, and I loved Vince, but I suppose I will never know what I missed getting married so young. I lost touch with my high school friends, and I only knew my college friends for a short time."

"Right," he said. At that he lifted his glass to mine and looked into my eyes as he said, "Here's to new beginnings, for both of us."

"Hear, hear," I said, as we toasted one another.

At that, he put down his glass and said, "Hey, how about we take a swim? You up for that?" He tapped his hands on his thighs like he was playing the drums.

"Sure," I said, without hesitation.

"Let's do it then."

He took off his shirt and his rock-solid abs looked tan and lean. I took off my top and shorts and felt very relaxed in my bikini. He started to put the ladder down for me to go in, but I surprised him and jumped off the side.

"Okay! Now I see the real Clair Bondi," he said, laughing, and jumped in after me.

We laughed and swam around a bit. With all the salt in the water, it was easy to stay afloat. It felt marvelous. We moved back and forth treading water, bobbing and weaving as we felt the warmth of the sea and the glow of the setting sun. After making our way back to the boat and up the ladder, Leon got some towels. We tied them around our waists and unexpectedly turned toward one another, face to face. Without hesitation, he put his arms around me. I leaned in to him, and it felt so natural to have him kiss me. First it was quick, and then it was long.

He pulled me back and stared into my eyes. "Clair," he said, "you are so beautiful." He kissed me again, as his tongue gently, yet passionately, seduced my mouth. I was afraid he could feel my heart racing. I craved his touch. I wanted him to go further. He pulled back again as if to ask if it was okay. I suppose my eyes gave him the answer. I remembered the scene in *Bridges of Madison County* when Clint Eastwood said to Francesca, "If you want me to stop, tell me now."

He took me by my arm and led me downstairs through the kitchen to one of the closed doors. When he opened it, there was a bedroom with a skylight that went to the deck above. The room was turquoise blue. The bed was all white with a white quilted upholstered headboard. There were pieces of modern art in silver frames with wide white mats, and each one had a pop of color in the center that looked like a squiggly line—one was orange, one was red, one was yellow, and one was navy blue. They were quite large and each went from the floor to the ceiling. It could have been an art gallery.

We stood by the bed as his lips moved across mine, and his hands caressed my body. He kissed my neck and then my lips. He took off my towel, and he took off his. He ran his hands over my breasts pulling down the straps of my bikini and lifted my arms. He caressed my nipples.

We fell to the bed. He was forceful in a gentle way. He took his time, caressing my body from head to toe. Neither of us said a word. It felt all-encompassing as he thrust himself atop me. We fell into a natural rhythm and made love with tireless energy.

Soon after, he lay on his side with his arms around me, and I began to fight back tears. "What's wrong, Clair?" he asked. I thought maybe he was worried he had moved too quickly—having sex too soon after Vince's death.

"I can't believe what just happened," I said, as I looked into his eyes. "I've never been with anyone but Vince."

"Seriously?" His head moved back a bit away from me. He

seemed to be relieved that it had nothing to do with him, but at the same time, surprised by my revelation.

"There's a lot more to my story, Leon, which I will tell you later. Now isn't the time."

"There'll be plenty of time for that," he said, as he kissed me and held me tight. The waves gently rocked the yacht as dusk turned to night.

Chapter 16

I awoke with my eyes looking toward the ceiling through the skylight with the bright sun of the new day streaming down upon me. The recent memory of last night was foremost in my mind as I adjusted to where I was and the realization of what had happened. This was earth shattering. I couldn't believe what I had done. My God, this was so not me. This was stuff I had only read about in romance novels, not a married woman with children like me. But then again, I wasn't married anymore. Things were happening so fast.

Before I could think about it, I heard Leon walking on the deck above. I was nude, and as I started to get up, I saw there was a robe and a note at the bottom of the bed. *Everything's in the bathroom that you might need. Take your time. L.*

I went into the bathroom and took a shower. It, too, was all white with fluffy yellow towels. The warm water on my body felt soothing. He was right; everything was there: razor, shaving cream, shower gel, deodorant, toothpaste, toothbrush, and perfume. I had a feeling he was used to doing this sort of thing: bringing a woman on board, having sex, and then having her stay over. Why else would he have all this stuff? I didn't know enough about him, and suddenly I didn't feel so special. But I wanted the moment to be special. I was more confused than ever. Had I done the right thing?

I wore the robe, and, after quickly brushing my hair and locating my sunglasses, I ventured upstairs.

"Good morning," said Leon, enthusiastically, with a smile. He had on red shorts and a navy-blue polo. It looked like he had been doing some boat-related chores since he had a bucket in his hand. He set it down and came over to me and gave me a hug.

"Hi," I said, smiling coyly, as he wrapped his arms around me. He continued to hold me tight, shaking me a bit, as if to loosen me up a bit. We rocked each other side to side in each other's arms. Then he walked over to a small table and chairs.

"Come on over here and sit down. You must be hungry. I know I am." He had coffee, OJ, yogurt, fruit, and some cheese. "How'd you sleep?"

"I don't remember," I said, as I sat down on the deck chair.

"Well, then, it must have been good. I see you found the shower."

I tightened the tie to the very fine cotton robe. I had bought myself one similar to it when in Paris on Saint-Germaine-des-Prés. "Yes, so nice of you. You seem to have a way of thinking of everything. Leon," I started to say, and then stopped. He must have noticed that I felt a bit awkward.

"Clair, last night was great. Really, really, great."

"Yes, I know, that's for sure, but I wanted to explain a bit."

"You don't have to do any explaining to me."

"No, I need to, or rather, I should say, I want to."

"Okay, then, I'm all ears." He leaned back in his chair and

crossed his legs and picked up his coffee cup.

"I want to tell you something about my marriage. It wasn't what it may have appeared to be. Vince wasn't into me before he died. It was really hard. We went to therapy, counseling, several different times."

He didn't say anything, but I could tell that he was surprised. I think he didn't want to make a big deal over what I was saying and wanted me to feel comfortable.

"I felt lost—not like a woman anymore, and he just grew more and more distant. And, since he was the only man I'd ever been with, it was really emotional for me to be with you last night. It was more than just my being with another man. It was a lot of emotions tied up to the fact that I felt rejected for such a long time." I waited for him to respond.

When he thought it was appropriate to comment, he jumped in. "I'm surprised to hear that from you, Clair. I can't imagine in a million years why Vince wouldn't have wanted to be with you."

I had planned on telling him the whole story of the detective and the mistress, but at the last minute, I decided not to. My original belief that no one must know about the mistress in order to protect my daughters took precedence.

"I'm sorry, Clair, for the pain you endured over all of that. But I hope you realize you're a beautiful, kind woman who has a lot to offer a man, and any man in his right mind would want to be with you." He surely knew what to say. "Clair," he said, leaning forward and reaching for my hand, "since we're being honest with one another about our pasts, let me tell you something about my life that may help you.

"My marriage was far from perfect. As I had told you, Jan was bipolar, but there was another problem. She cheated on me. I was hurt and angry, but I stayed for Ethan's sake. Looking back, I'm glad I did, considering their tragic deaths. But, as sad as all that was, and will always be, I found that life goes on. I have had a few relationships that I have really enjoyed. I've since realized that I was sacrificing an awful lot by staying with a woman who wasn't honest with me and didn't give me the respect I should have been given. No one can live like that."

I couldn't believe what he was saying. It was my life he was speaking of, but I couldn't tell him. I continued to listen.

"Living with someone who isn't meeting your needs or who is causing you heartache isn't worth staying for if you've tried to fix it."

Oh, how right he was. "I'm sorry to hear that, Leon."

"So," he said, standing up and taking my hand into his and wrapping my arm around his waist, "Clair Bondi, we need to get back. I've got to get to the office. But will you have dinner with me tonight up at Amanyara? My buddy's the chef up there, and I'll have him plant us a table in the sand under the stars."

"Leon, I like your style," I said.

"How about I pick you up at eight?"

"Perfect."

"Let's get going." At that he went into full captain mode, commanding the yacht as we headed back to the other side of Provo.

Chapter 17

I hadn't looked at my phone since I left the house the night before. There were several text messages, as well as concerned phone calls from both Emilie and Reese because of their inability to reach me.

Message from Reese: "Mom, please call me. Where are you?"

Message from Emilie: "Mom, I'm really getting concerned about you. This isn't like you. Reese and I are getting worried. Please call."

I immediately called each of them and made up an excuse that I had turned my phone off because I had gone to bed early. I wasn't sure they would buy that since they both knew that I was a night owl. I was glad that I got their voicemails rather than having to talk.

I flopped onto my bed as if I were doing a back dive and spread my arms out above my shoulders. I couldn't help but smile. I felt great. Leon had awakened a part of me that had lain dormant for so many years. Regardless of what our relationship might become, that fact was certain, and I was so appreciative. I decided not to worry about Leon's past relationships, particularly those that had been on the island, and enjoy the moment.

The next two weeks were days and nights of complete and total bliss—romantic dinners, wonderful sex, and great conversation. We danced around my living room to the music of Steve Tyrell for hours upon end, embracing one another, sipping champagne. We dined at the most fabulous restaurants of Provo—Amanyara for a mouth-watering steak, Parallel 23 for succulent lobster, and Anacaona for the best grilled tuna. Karen and Paul Newman (no, not the actor), the owners of Coyaba, my all-time favorite, were surprised to see us together. They were saddened to hear about Vince, but they were happy that "two great people had found one another." They sent over dessert—their famous apple tart sprinkled with powdered sugar and topped with vanilla ice cream—the most delicious dessert I had ever tasted in all of my travels.

We got couple's massages at the Spa at the Regent Palms and in the cozy pitched-ceiling hut on the beach at Point Grace, where the white curtains blew in the gentle indigenous breeze of Turks and Caicos.

We talked about every subject under the sun—sports, politics, world peace, theater, music, and the latest gadgets (he was a huge Apple fan and had every product they made, always the newest version). He always ended the night by saying, "Clair Bondi, how did I ever get so lucky?" We made plans for him to come to Philadelphia, where we would go to New York and to some of my favorite places—the Carlyle to hear Steve Tyrell and catch a Broadway show with dinner at Le Bernardin beforehand.

And then I got the phone call from Detective Martin that I had been anticipating. They were about to arrest the young man he had told me about. While they had been following this "person of interest" for the last two weeks, they suddenly saw him, just the day before, wearing a white gold Rolex watch. When they brought him in for questioning, they asked him about it, and he told them he found it. That location was in the same vicinity where Vince and his Porsche were found. The watch had the initials *VJB* engraved on the back. They felt they had their man.

My feeling of optimism that they would get this young man to confess, especially since he already had a record, was a welcome relief. I knew it was time for me to fly back to Philadelphia, although I didn't want to leave. Leon, also sad, was happy that this would finally be over for me. Even though I had no idea how long it would take for the arrest and sentencing, I felt good about moving toward resolution. I was looking forward to putting it behind me.

I awoke to my phone buzzing with a text from Captain Martin. "FYI—Calvin Howard, twenty-three, of West Philadelphia, rough background, has just been arrested and is currently being booked. Will be on news tonight."

I responded, "Flying back today. Will be home by 6:00 p.m."

And then another from Captain Martin: "Will contact you later this evening to fill you in."

And then me: "Thank you."

So there it was. A twenty-three-year-old's life was about to change. It was crazy to me that he could have served time as an accomplice for another murder and that he would do something so horrible. I remember taking a social work class in college about the cycle of crime in families. It sounded like this was the same thing: kids who live a life where crime is part of it; kids who come home to a mother doing drugs and a father in jail or no father around at all. How could these kids have a chance? I found myself feeling sorry for this young man, as bizarre as that seemed.

How different his life must have been from my girls growing up, where their every need was taken care of and they had a loving family, great friends, and most importantly, opportunity, which this young man obviously didn't have. It also made me think of Ursula, who came from a similar background, yet she was making something of herself. I needed to call her. I wanted to talk with Leon about Ursula finding her daughter since he was adopted. He would be a good place to start.

I had so many ideas and thoughts racing through my head. I had to call the girls and let them know that I was on my way home and that the suspect was in custody.

Chapter 18

There wasn't much to do that morning before my flight. I was having a car pick me up. Leon wanted to take me, but I insisted on going myself. I didn't want to disrupt his day. Charles would pick me up in Philly.

I packed a carry-on soft bag with a book and a few magazines for the flight. The car came right on time, and before I knew it, I was at the airport. Families and couples were lined up to check in. The airport had just finished some major construction, which was greatly needed. Before the construction, everyone was huddled into a small waiting room for their flights, and it was difficult to get a seat. Now, there was plenty of room. They had added more duty-free shops, which I normally would have loved to have checked out, but I just didn't have it in me.

I didn't want to leave, and I didn't want to face what was next. I wanted to be back on Leon's yacht with him, making love under the stars and feeling the gentle breeze upon my body. All I could think about was how exciting and wonderful it felt to be with him. I never could have imagined feeling this great with a man, any man. As I waited for my plane, the family sitting across from me was eating hot dogs and drinking sodas, making a mess, and one of the kids spilled his drink. The father, in a huff, raced to the concession counter and grabbed some napkins. The mother just sat there, unfazed. Another couple, possibly going home from their honeymoon, sat gazing into each other's eyes and kissing, oblivious to the voyeurs.

Once I was on the plane, the takeoff from Turks was always bittersweet, even when I was there with Vince. Soaring into the sky over a view of the blue water was so breathtaking. I never tired of it. It always brought me such joy but also sadness that I was leaving. I was grateful that I didn't have to sell Blakely House. It was just unbelievable that it had worked out. This really was my place, a place like no other. My chance encounter with Leon changed my life in so many ways.

Once boarded and settled in, I had a glass of Chardonnay and listened to some music on my phone—Lionel Richie and Rod Stewart. I never opened my book. After landing, Charles was waiting for me downstairs from the terminal. His big smile greeted me as I descended the escalator. Several drivers were holding signs for people they were picking up. Charles stood off to the side. He was such a sweet man and had been married to his wife for fifty years.

"Clair, great to see you," he said, as he took my bag from me. No matter how small or large, he always took my bag. He certainly didn't need to carry this one, but I didn't object because I knew he would want to carry it.

"Hello, Charles, nice to see you, too."

"Good trip?" he asked.

"Yes, Charles, good trip."

"Clair," he said, with some hesitation, "I'm glad they got the guy who killed Vince."

"Yes, Charles, so am I."

So now it was all over the news, obviously. I knew I had to call the girls first thing when I got home, and that I did. Luckily, I was able to reach both of them. They were relieved and wanted to come home, but I told them to stay put and keep studying. They were in the midst of final exams and would be home in just a few days anyhow for the summer. They normally would have plans by now for summer jobs, but with all that had happened and the killer's trial to begin shortly, they wanted to be at home with me, for which I was thankful.

Barb and Jack called on speakerphone and offered to come over, but I told them I was fine and would rather go to bed and deal with things in the morning. I didn't watch the evening news and got to bed by nine. I tossed and turned all night. I had the alarm system on but heard every sound that a house makes in the middle of the night—or possibly that my imagination made. I was relieved to see the light of day, even though I was very tired from not sleeping. I fell asleep for a few hours and awoke around nine to the phone, and this time, it was Leon.

"Clair," he said, with intensity in his voice, "I have to talk to you. Can you talk right now?"

I sat up in bed, uncertain of what he was about to say.

"Yes, yes, Leon. I can talk."

"Clair, we got a phone call this morning from a woman identifying herself as Clair Bondi asking for the $8 million, saying she's coming in to pick up the money."

"What?" I said, blurting out my response.

"Yes, you heard me right. There's a woman saying she's you, and she wants to come in for the money that's in your account. She requested a bearer bond."

"Bearer bond? What is that?" I asked.

"It's like a check, but it isn't made out to anyone. Anyone can deposit it anywhere, and there's no way to track it."

I didn't understand how that could be, but I decided to let it ride and deal with finding out more about the woman. "Did you speak with her?"

"Yes, I did. When a request for withdrawal is anything that large, I have to speak to the person."

"What is her phone number?"

"I can't tell you that."

"Leon, we have to find out who it is. You have to tell me. I might recognize the number."

"Clair, by law, I can't reveal the number, but the number was blocked, so I don't know it either. This has to be handed over to the authorities here in Turks and Caicos. This is out of my jurisdiction at this point. Whenever something happens that we know is improper or not as it should be, particularly something where I know it isn't you, we have to alert the authorities."

"Oh, God, Leon. What the hell is going on?" I started to break down.

"Clair, I know you're upset to hear this, but we'll get to the bottom of it. Obviously, there is someone who knows about the money and is trying to get it. Vince could have shared this with someone. But with this type of situation, these people, or this person, are no amateurs. To try and extort $8 million is serious business. Did Vince have any business associates that could have known about this money?"

"Well, I think it's pretty strange that his accountant—our accountant—never mentioned it to me, as I had shared with you. I would have thought he must have known about it. But you said it was a woman who called, not a man."

"We don't know who is behind all of this. It could be a whole professional extortion scheme, whereby they have the woman call to impersonate you, take over your identity, and come in and take out the money, but someone else could be behind it. You never know. People come into banks trying to take people's money all the time or act like they're someone else to try to borrow money. That happens a lot, too."

"Good God."

"The authorities will have to investigate everything now. They will certainly want to speak to you. I'll call the necessary people within the bank, and they will take it from there. Clair, don't say a word to anyone—not even your daughters or your close friends. I'll be in touch. Miss you."

He sounded like he needed to get off the phone. "Miss you, too."

My thoughts initially turned to Kevin Marks. I didn't know that much about him because Vince handled all the money and our income taxes with Kevin. I only signed on the line when it came time to file. Even though I was making millions of dollars developing real estate, Vince handled that money, too. I did think it was strange when I had met with Kevin and our attorney, Bill Kaplan, that there wasn't as much money as I had thought there was. Vince never mentioned any problems with money. It just didn't add up. But one thing was for sure: Vince hadn't leveled with me on both fronts—his affair with Catherine or our financial situation. But the money was bothering me more at this point and really scaring me. Was Vince involved in other things he didn't tell me about? Could he have been involved with some Mafia-type people who were getting back at him now? It made me think of the girls when they were in high school. One day Emilie came home from school crying because some of the kids said we were in the Mafia. Of course, I thought it was ridiculous and laughed it off. But maybe it was true?

And then I got to thinking about Bill Kaplan. I had a little more involvement with him, since we used to go out with him and his wife, Gayle. But after their divorce, we didn't go out any longer. Vince did say that Bill ran around. In hindsight, Vince used to talk about several men that we knew running around. That certainly was the pot calling the kettle black.

And then it hit me: *OMG, Catherine Rogers.* Could it be Catherine? Would Vince have shared the information about the secret account in Turks with her? And would she even have the ability to risk taking out the $8 million, especially with her young daughter? Surely, she wouldn't have thought she could pull off something as clandestine as that. Even Leon had said this would have had to be a professional. Leon also said that the woman was going to come into the bank to get the money herself. If it were Catherine, I would certainly be able to identify her. Even though I had never met her, there were many photos of her online.

Or maybe it was the jeweler, Tina Rorer. She was crazy. She even came to our house one day after Vince had ended the affair. I was in the backyard planting tomato plants, and Vince was in the garage. She came walking down our driveway yelling at him and calling him awful names. He had to take ahold of her and bring her back up to her car and drive her around until she calmed down. Thank God the girls weren't at home.

Bottom line, this was major. I really didn't think either of them would do such a thing, but I've been wrong about things in the past. But one thing I knew for sure: I wasn't going to say anything about my thoughts regarding Catherine or Tina. That was one subject I wasn't going to discuss with Leon. That information would stay in the vault.

I decided I had to wait and see what the authorities found out. Luckily, I had Leon. I couldn't help but think what might have happened if I hadn't met him. This person could have gotten all the money, and I would have never known about it.

Then another scenario came into focus. I had been the victim of identity theft two years before when my wallet was stolen in New York City. I was walking from Fekkai to Bergdorf's for lunch, and while I was holding up my umbrella, a woman bumped into my right side. I discovered after lunch when I went to pay that I was missing my wallet.

I was able to pay for lunch on my charge that they looked up, but I had to have my stylist lend me some cash to get a train ticket home. After filing several reports about the incident, I found out that a few months later a woman walked into a branch of my bank in North Carolina and took out $10,000 from my account. To make matters worse, she then went to another branch twenty minutes away and took out another $10,000. Neither teller bothered to look at the signature card. The woman didn't even have my account number initially, but since she somehow got my social security number and told the teller the number. The first teller looked up my account number. It was the second teller who went to her supervisor after she had given away the second $10,000 and felt uneasy about it. The supervisor called me and asked me if I had been banking in North Carolina. I told her that I most certainly had not.

It turned out it was a crime ring. They had a system where one person would bump into you and another would come on the other side and dip into your handbag. There was a trial, and they were now serving jail time. I was asked to testify, but I passed. I didn't need crooks knowing anything else about me. I wondered if these criminals could have somehow gotten information about the money in Turks. Even though they were serving jail time, maybe they had given this information to someone else on the outside. That happened frequently.

I knew I had to keep this to myself and wait to see what the authorities found out. But regardless of what they would discover, I just hoped I could hold it all together.

Chapter 19

There were other things happening that had to get taken care of, despite what was going on with the suspect under arrest and the Turks and Caicos police work regarding the woman impersonating me.

The oceanfront house at the beach was just about completed, but my builder called to tell me that we forgot something really important—an outdoor shower. I couldn't believe that the architect, the builder, and I missed it, but we did. Now we had to figure out where to put it when we had no more impervious coverage available. The borough was really strict about that, and the building inspector would notice it if we put the shower in then. Luckily, we had built a pool house, so I turned the changing room into a shower. We had already roughed in the plumbing in case the owner decided to put in a sink or commode afterward. We decided to have the last inspection before settlement and then put the shower in afterward.

Sam was going to handle everything, for which I was

grateful. He had taken up a lot of the slack while I was dealing with Vince's death and being away so much. He was a really good guy—single, around forty-five, lived for the beach. As long as he had his surfboard, he was happy. I often wondered what he did with his money since he was the best builder in the area and had to be making a ton.

I had a slew of phone calls from friends and relatives—my mom, Vince's sister, neighbors, my tennis group, and Vince's tennis group. Everyone was saying the same thing: "At least now it will be over," "The guy's got a record," "He was wearing Vince's watch," "He was right where Vince was shot," "You'll be able to go on with your life." I wish I believed that, but with the secret money, I knew a lot more was to come regardless of who killed Vince.

Captain Martin also called to tell me that Calvin would be held for trial. He revealed the young man had an alibi—a friend Calvin claimed to be "hanging out with" that night. The friend confirmed it, but the detective also said that meant nothing. The friend had a record, too, for theft. He also told me to "sit tight" and let the process take place. I told him I would.

So, I had everything I could possibly do at that moment under control. And then an unexpected happy occurrence: Ursula was at my side door holding a plant. I sprinted to open the door, and it was really nice to see her.

She had just graduated, and she wanted to let me know how much she appreciated my friendship. She was to begin her new job at Campbell Soup the next day, and she had just bought a used car and wanted to show it to me. Of course, I ran outside and gushed over it. It was a white Toyota with a black interior, and she was so proud. It took my mind off of things for a bit. I invited her in, but she had to get going. We decided to meet again soon. I was going to tell her about Leon and being adopted and how we could go forward with finding her daughter, but I thought it could wait. This moment for which she had worked so hard—to finish college and buy her own car—had to be celebrated on its own without anything else clouding the joy.

I spent the next few days at home catching up on mail, taking walks, and entertaining some visitors who came to see how I was doing. Barb and Jack brought dinner over one night—pot roast in a thick gravy with potatoes and carrots. I usually ate much lighter, but I really enjoyed it, and it was nice to be with them.

But then, after several days of waiting to find out who the woman was who had called Leon and if she came to get the money, I felt like I was going to explode. I called him early one morning. I hadn't heard from him since he first called me with the shocking development.

"Clair, I can't talk to you about this right now. The T&C police and customs departments have demanded that I do not talk about the case with you, but please know that they are on top of everything."

"Why can't you tell me who it is? I won't say anything to anyone."

There was dead silence.

"Leon, I'm talking to you!" I shouted.

"Clair, please calm down. Please."

"I thought we had something going between us, but obviously not," I said abruptly.

"Clair, my phone could be tapped for all I know. The authorities could be listening to our conversation right at this very moment. I have disclosed my relationship with you to them, both personal and business. I had to do that. I must stay out of this right now. Not for always, but for now. And you must stay out of it, too. You could jeopardize the case. They know what they are doing. Let things play out. They will contact you when they are ready to disclose what's going on."

"Then just stay out of it," I said, abruptly. And I hung up the phone.

Even Leon had let me down. He should have trusted me enough to tell me. I didn't care about the police or anyone else. I thought the trust we shared was more important than anything I should or shouldn't be doing with the authorities.

I took a deep breath and decided I had to be honest with the girls and tell them what was happening when they arrived home on Monday. They were headed home for summer break. This was too big for me to handle myself. This was like being underwater without an oxygen tank.

I was so naïve. When they talk about flaws in people, that would be mine. A simple summation that should be etched on my tombstone: Clair Bondi, guilty of naiveté. What a fool I was about Vince, my lawyer, and my accountant. People do what they need to do for their own gain. Those professionals handling our assets had to have known that something was going on. I found it hard to believe that they didn't. But they were getting paid a lot of money to handle things for us, so I'm sure they overlooked it if Vince told them to.

I had to focus on Reese and Emilie. They were my top priority. They didn't deserve to have to deal with all of this. We would make it through. I knew that we would. But what would happen before the end, I didn't know. We had to deal with the murder trial, and now the unknown of who tried to take out the money was driving me crazy. If it was one of the mistresses, everyone would find out, and everyone who felt sorry for Vince and his murder would know what he really was all about—a man who let down his wife and his daughters in disgrace.

My phone rang again. It was Leon. I didn't answer, but instead, put it on vibrate. I couldn't deal with him or anyone else. I was on meltdown.

And then I heard a knock. I got off the kitchen barstool and walked to the side door. There were two men standing there. I opened the door, and they flashed their shiny badges that were inside black wallets. They both flipped them open at the same time.

"Mrs. Bondi," said the one agent, "we're with the United States Customs Department, and we need to speak with you. May we come in?"

"Yes, come in," I said, softly. I walked them into the kitchen where they sat down at the table. They didn't have anything with them—no briefcases or folders of any sort.

"Mrs. Bondi, I'm Agent Frank Ramsey, and this is my colleague, Agent Mike Mattius. We need to talk to you about a Kristee Adams. Do you know a woman by the name of Kristee Adams?"

"Sure, she's my husband's assistant, for work—or rather, was his assistant. Did something happen to her?"

"Mrs. Bondi, let's back up a second, if we could. Let me first say, we are aware of your relationship with Mr. Leon Abramson of First Caribbean Bank and that you were made aware of $8 million in an account that you had no previous knowledge of prior to your late husband's death. Is that correct?"

"Yes, that is correct." I couldn't imagine why they would be talking about Kristee. Maybe she told them something about Vince that led them to the person trying to take out the money.

"Okay, we're on the same page then. And we were also told by Mr. Abramson that a woman had contacted the bank acting as you with regard to withdrawing the eight million and that he had told you by phone about the woman's phone call. Is that also correct?"

"Yes, it is, but he never told me who it was."

"Yes, we understand. As a result of this information reported by Mr. Abramson, the call was traced to a Kristee Adams. We followed her to Turks and Caicos, in cooperation with the Turks and Caicos police and customs agents, whereby she tried to assume your identity and take out the money at the office of Mr. Leon Abramson of First Caribbean Bank."

I could feel the blood from my body rushing to my head. I tried to focus.

"She is now in custody in a Turks and Caicos prison—Her Majesty's Prison to be exact, on Grand Turk—and from there will go back to Providenciales for a hearing before their Supreme Court, awaiting arraignment for extortion and trying to assume the identity of another person for that purpose."

"Supreme Court?" I asked.

"They do things a little differently down there than we do here in the States. Their Supreme Court isn't the final stop; it's where people go who do serious felony-type offenses like Ms. Adams has done." And then came the kicker: "Mrs. Bondi, is there anything we should know about your husband's relationship with Ms. Adams?"

"Relationship?" I asked, unclear as to what they meant by that comment.

"Yes," they said, looking at one another.

My God, were they assuming they had more than a working relationship?

"No, no," I said, turning my head from side to side. "She only worked for him. She was just his assistant. She handled all the administrative stuff—typing, computer work, and stuff like that. I hardly knew her. She's been so nice ever since Vince died. She's young—like thirty years old."

"Mrs. Bondi, we don't know what their relationship was. We just need to ask these questions. We don't mean to upset you."

"Right, right," I said, getting my composure back a bit.

"Mrs. Bondi, that is all we will need for right now. I do want you to know that Mr. Abramson is the only other person aware of this information at this point. He had been advised not to talk to you about it. But you may speak with him about it now that she is in custody. You are free to talk to your family, but we would appreciate you not talking with the media, should this information be released."

"I understand." I could feel my body shaking.

And then the other officer spoke. "Mrs. Bondi, we regret that we had to come here today to your home and tell you all of this. We know that you have been dealing with the fatal shooting of your husband, and we can only imagine that hearing this has got to be difficult for you. Please accept our condolences."

"Thank you."

"Is there anyone you could have come over and stay with you or a place you could go for tonight? It might be best not to be by yourself."

"I'll see. Yes, thanks," I said, half-heartedly.

At that, they stood up and walked to the side door. I followed behind them in silence.

Agent Ramsey took his card from his wallet and handed it to me. "Call me anytime. We just wanted to let you know what is going on and the current status. Again, sorry for all of this."

"Thank you."

Chapter 20

I watched as they pulled away in their black Ford SUV. No one would know who they were, I thought, as they backed out of the driveway. No one would know that my life was just brought to an even lower level than the day Vince was shot.

After hearing what they had to say about Leon and his order not to contact me, I realized I had been too hard on him. I picked up my phone and called him, leaving a short message to call me when he could and telling him that the agents had been here. I wasn't sure what to do next. I really wanted to talk to Leon first. I needed him more than I realized. I was afraid after the way I had talked to him that I wouldn't hear from him again.

I was about to walk upstairs when I heard the side doorbell ring. I certainly wasn't in any mood to entertain any guests or relatives. I also thought maybe it was the agents returning, for whatever reason. Maybe they had to ask me something else. I walked from the foyer to the kitchen and looked toward the side door. I couldn't believe my eyes! It was Leon. How on earth could he be here? He stood looking through the glass panes with the biggest smile on his face. I couldn't get to the door fast enough.

I opened the door and leaped into Leon's arms, almost knocking him over as we struggled to get inside. I wouldn't let go of him. "Leon, Leon, I can't believe you're here!" I said, in complete shock, as I finally leaned back to look at his face. "I just called you, thinking you were in Turks at the bank. I can't believe you're here! Oh my God!"

His dark eyes were so comforting and mysterious at the same time. "I know, but I wanted to be nearby to come over as soon as the customs agents told you about everything. I worked out an arrangement that they would call me after they met with you."

"But where were you?"

"I was overnight at the Marriott in Conshohocken. They literally called me fifteen minutes ago."

"I can't believe you did that for me." I hugged him again, burying my head into his neck.

He pulled me back so he could see my face and said, "Well, it's all over now. I'm sorry, Clair. I really, really am sorry for what you have been through and what you will be going through with all of this, in addition to the trial for the guy who killed Vince."

I started to cry and pulled my hands up to cover my face. "How did she pull all of this off? Kristee Adams? Of all people." We sat down at the barstools at the kitchen island.

"Almost pulled off. She went through customs as herself, but when she came to my office, she had all fake documents."

"All things with my name on them?"

"Yes, she was thorough—passport, birth certificate, social security card, driver's license. She had this all planned out."

"I can't imagine her sitting in your office acting like she was me."

As much as I was curious to ask how she handled herself, I

didn't want to know. It was frightening to think of someone assuming your identity to steal from you. I couldn't go there to ask for any more details.

"Well, she sure did, and now she will have to pay the price," he said.

"Yes, the agents explained the process to me—her being in jail and awaiting a trial."

There was silence for a moment, and I saw a look on Leon's face that was serious, yet uncertain. He looked into my eyes, then looked straight ahead away from me. He seemed like he wanted to say more, but yet he wasn't sure what to say. I had never seen him look like that.

"Clair, let's talk." He took my hand, and we walked into the family room and sat down on the sofa. "Listen," he said, as he put his arm around me and looked into my eyes, "I want to be here for you. You're going to need support. I love you. I have never met anyone like you. I have some vacation time coming to me, and I would like to spend it with you, helping in any way that I can. Please allow me to do that for you."

I knew that I needed Leon. "I love you, too." Leon was sent right from heaven. There was no doubt about that. "It's just that I have so much that I have to tell Emilie and Reese," I said. "They don't even know about you. I have no idea what their reaction will be when I tell them that I fell in love with my banker, let alone the secret money, and now Kristee assuming my identity and the trial. I'm afraid this will be too much for them. I'm scared, Leon. So very, very scared."

"You have a right to be scared. But one thing you have to remember: what you have been through and what you have been able to face straight on and get resolved so far is admirable. Your daughters will respect you for that."

"I know you're right, but I worry so much about them. They

might hate me and never understand how we met and our relationship. Their father just died, and their mother has a boyfriend? What mother does something like that?"

"They may not understand everything right now at this very moment, but they will. You have to concentrate on what needs to get done now. You have to get the business stuff straightened out. Have you connected with the man who owns part of the company? What's his name?"

"Jim Stone. No, I haven't. My accountant and lawyer said he would handle everything and that I could contact him when I was ready. He wasn't able to come to Vince's funeral because his mother had just died, so I haven't seen him."

"Well, you're going to have to tell him about Kristee. Clair, I'm pretty certain there could be more to all of this about Kristee."

I knew what he was suggesting. I couldn't bring myself to believe it when the customs agents asked me.

"Do you think something was going on between them?" he asked.

"Absolutely not," I said. "She's so young."

"So? What's that got to do with it?"

And then I thought I should level with him. "Leon, Vince had two affairs—one with our jeweler eight years ago and one with a consultant from Los Angeles just recently. I had him followed by a detective just before he was shot."

"So that's what you had been dealing with, and you never told me."

"Yes, that's right."

"Clair, whatever went on with the two of them, you haven't done anything wrong. Remember that. Husbands who are connected with their wives—husbands who share financial information—don't behave the way Vince did and set up secret accounts. Kristee knew about the money. How and why she knew about it, we don't know yet. But we will. There's a good chance that Vince was preparing to divorce you. He just wanted to get a large chunk of money put away that you wouldn't know about. Men don't like to split up their money, and that's most likely why the account was set up." I was quiet, trying to take it all in. Then Leon changed the subject, probably thinking I was overwhelmed. "When do your daughters come home?"

"Tomorrow."

"Okay then. We have one night. One night it is. Let's have some fun." He pulled me up off the sofa. "What do you want to do?"

"I just want to be with you," I said, wiping my eyes.

"How about if we stay in and order some food and have some wine? By the way, your home is beautiful, which I knew it would be." He walked toward the French doors of the living room, opened one side, and took a look at the piano. "Gorgeous. Love it," he said, as he sat down and his hands tickled the keys. And then he started to play and sing Jennifer Hudson's song from *Dreamgirls*. "One night only, one night only . . ."

And then I sang, "Come on, big baby, come on . . ." I loved that he knew about music and theater. He was so exciting. I couldn't stop smiling. After what had just transpired, it was hard to believe I was actually having fun.

He pulled me down onto his lap and kissed me. "Have you got any champagne?" He kissed me again.

"I always have champagne."

He kissed me again. "Great. One night only . . ."

And what a night it was. He didn't have anything with him, since he had reserved his room at the Marriott for the next week and all his stuff was there. But he didn't stay there that night, that one night only. We ordered a pizza, drank champagne, danced to Lionel Richie, laughed, talked, and fell into the same rhythm we had going in Turks when we spent the night under a full moon making love on his yacht. For one night I put everything aside, despite what I would have to face the next day.

Chapter 21

It was still dark when I awoke. For an instant, my mind was blank before the reality of yesterday sunk in. And for a second, I didn't even realize that Leon was there with me. As he lay next to me, I couldn't help but wonder how this mess I found myself in would affect our relationship. Would he grow tired of all the stress? I wouldn't want to have to deal with it all if he were the one in the same situation. I truly believed he was sincere about wanting to stand by me in all of this, but I found it almost too good to be true.

I looked over at him as he slept. His overnight facial hair was apparent, making him appear even sexier, if that were possible. His hair was tousled from lying down, and even with his eyelids closed, he looked hot. Knowing that he was nude underneath the duvet cover was an erotic thought. I had put on a short black slip after we had finished having sex, but he stayed commando.

It felt strange to have a man in the bed I'd shared with Vince, but it felt good—although different. For one thing, we had sex.

My eyes glanced upon his belt that was lying on the side chair. It was the same one that Vince had—the silver Tiffany belt buckle with his initials engraved: *LSA*. It seemed that all successful, well-dressed men had that same belt buckle. I would have to ask him his middle name.

"Hey," he said, as he awoke and put his arm around me, pulling me close. "Good morning. Are you okay?"

"I don't know how to answer that." I nudged my head under his arm, leaning on his chest. I could feel the warmth of his breath.

"It's got to be hard. But you're going to get through it. You've already made a lot of headway—the guy's in jail for killing Vince, and Kristee's in custody for assuming your identity and trying to get the money. A lot has already been figured out."

"I know."

"Now, with regard to your daughters, I don't want to be in the way, so you tell me how you want to handle that. I'll be over at the Marriott, and you just call me when you need me. I'm here for a week. Whatever works for you."

He began to get up but fell back onto the bed and stared into my eyes as he lay upon me. Neither of us said anything. He was aroused, and so was I. We took advantage of the moment, both in bed and then again in the shower. *God, please let it always be like this.*

I wanted to make him breakfast, but he insisted on leaving to go back to the hotel so I could do what I needed to do. Charles would be picking up the girls from the airport around six that evening. I normally would have arranged to ride along with Charles to meet them, but I didn't think I could emotionally hide my feelings with what I had to tell them about Kristee. Their flights were scheduled to come in around the same time, which worked out well. The weather was a bit ominous with high winds and a heavy downpour, and it was supposed to be that way all day.

I was hoping they would be able to land okay in Philly.

I decided, unexpectedly, to send a text to Sheryl Meister, the former FBI agent who had recommended the detective when I had Vince followed, to ask her for another recommendation—a forensic accountant. I first heard about forensic accountants while watching an episode of *Law & Order: Special Victims Unit*. And I thought that I was surely a person who could use one to check out all that I didn't know about our finances and investments. She wrote back immediately with a recommendation: Jane Alexander, Forensic Accountant, with her phone number.

Okay. It was now or never. I picked up the phone and dialed. To my surprise, she answered after the first ring. I explained my situation. I was surprised and caught a bit off guard when she told me she could meet in just two hours. I didn't think it would be so soon. I decided to get the process started and agreed to meet at Vince's office.

Next, I called Jim Stone and got him on the first ring, as well. I explained what was going on with Kristee. He didn't seem that shocked, or at least he didn't let on that he knew about anything. He didn't give me any trouble with my bringing in a forensic accountant and told me to do whatever was needed. He even told me where everything was, both personal and business. I was surprised that he was so cooperative. I sometimes forgot that I owned just as much of the business as Vince, even though I didn't run it, so I felt like I wasn't necessarily privy to the information. I was relieved that I didn't get emotional on the call; I just gave him the information. After I hung up, I took a deep breath and got myself ready to go to the office.

And then I got two text messages from the girls:

"Mom, can't wait to see you. I want to be there for whatever you need with the trial. xo Em."

"Mom, I will feel so much better when I can see you and we

can all get through this together. Love you. R."

Luckily, I had to leave right away to meet with the forensic accountant, so I didn't have time to think about what I needed to tell them.

I drove to the office. No one was there since it was a Saturday, which was good. I was about ten minutes early, so I started going through the files where all the cancelled checks were and all of Vince's personal and business American Express statements. Everything was in order.

I heard a car pull up and saw a tiny woman in a white shirt and black pants, about sixty years old, get out of a white Audi. She had shiny gray hair pulled back in a neatly knotted bun. I walked to the door and greeted her.

"Hello, I'm Clair."

"Hello, Clair. Jane Alexander," she said, reaching for my hand.

"Please, come in. Thanks for coming out today without really any notice."

"I was free, so I thought it would be good to come."

We went into Vince's office, and I sat behind the desk and she sat on a chair facing me. I thought of all the times I sat in that same chair when I went to Vince's office for one thing or another.

"First, let me say, I am so sorry to hear of the loss of your husband," she said, as she got out her legal pad from her briefcase.

"Thank you. I'm dealing with much more than the loss of my husband at the moment, unfortunately. "

"I understand."

"Not only was my husband fatally shot and a trial is about to get started, but his assistant, Kristee Adams, tried to assume my identity to take money from an account in Turks and Caicos that I never knew about."

She sighed and rolled her eyes.

"Worse yet, I didn't even know about the account until Leon

Abramson, president of the First Caribbean Bank of Turks and Caicos, told me about it. I hadn't even known him, either. He happened to come to my home in Turks to express his condolences. It's a long story, but that's about it in a nutshell."

"Do you know the reason you were not aware of the account?"

"I thought originally, when I first found out about the $8 million, that it was because Vince might have thought I wouldn't agree with his putting money there to hide it from the IRS. But then, when the Turks and Caicos police and customs agents arrested Kristee Adams for stealing my identity and trying to take out the money in person, I realized that might not be the reason."

"Mrs. Bondi, husbands hide money from their wives for a multitude of reasons. You wouldn't be the first whose husband had another relationship to hide."

"I don't know for certain right now if there was any other relationship between them other than business. Right before my husband was shot, he was having an affair with someone else, and he had done that once before, several years ago."

At that, she shifted her body in her chair and sat up taller. "Okay, then, I assume you want me to look over the books and see what's there and report back to you on anything that doesn't appear to be as it should be."

"Yes, that would be great. I have everything ready for you. Jim Stone, a partner in the company, is in full agreement about my handing this all over to you."

"Are you a partner in the company, as well?"

"Yes, Vince and I each own 37 percent, and Jim owns the rest."

"You do not need his permission, Mrs. Bondi." At that, she stood up and quickly looked at the pile of information.

"Everything here is for the last ten years—all the account numbers and the accounting, so if you have any questions, just call me."

"Okay. I will take a look, and if I need anything else, I'll let you know. I plan on working through the weekend, so I will call you on Monday with a preliminary report. We might have to dig deeper, but we'll see where it takes us. Each case is different. We'll get to a point whereby it isn't worth examining anything further. I will let you know."

This woman doesn't mess around. "Okay then. Thank you."

At that she put everything into two large blue and yellow bags that she had folded up in her handbag. She left, and I left, too. I had had enough for our first encounter. Something told me that Jane would find more things. What they would be, I had no idea, but with what had already taken place, I was trying to prepare myself for whatever she might find.

I drove home looking forward to seeing the girls, but at the same time, I was scared to see them. What should have been the anticipation of the beginning of a great summer before each of their final year of law school and medical school was instead the beginning of two trials.

I had about four hours before the girls would be home. I decided to make their favorite: nachos. I stopped at Whole Foods and bought the ingredients, and since I had some great red wine, which I knew we were going to need, I didn't have to stop at the liquor store.

As much as I was looking forward to having the girls back home, I couldn't help but think about Leon in his hotel room. I gave him a call and got him on the first ring.

"Hi," I said.

"Hey, there. How's it going?" He sounded like he had been sleeping.

"Just making some nachos for the girls when they get home."

"Sounds good."

"What are you doing?"

"Fell asleep watching the tennis match."

"Leon, I don't think it's fair for you to be here just waiting around for me to let you know when you can come over. I have no idea what's going to happen. I feel bad."

"Don't worry about it. Let's just wait and see."

"Are you sure?"

"Yes, I'm sure."

"Okay. I'll call you when I can."

"See ya. I'll be thinking of you, Clair. Love you."

"Love you, too."

Leon didn't go on and on about things. He was direct, yet kind. So many men talked so much about themselves. It was refreshing that he wasn't like that.

Just as I hung up, I saw headlights through the mudroom door to the driveway. The girls leaped from the side doors of Charles' car and came racing to the door. Tears started to flow down my face. They looked great with huge smiles on their faces. We all hugged and held on tight to one another.

"So wonderful to see you girls!"

"Nothing better than to see you, Mom," said Reese.

"Yes," added Emilie. "Smells good in here."

"I made nachos, so we can just have an easy, relaxing dinner. I'm sure you're both tired."

The conversation was light—the girls talked about their flights, and I was dying inside with deciding when was a good time to tell them about Kristee.

I took a bite of my nacho and then all of a sudden burst into tears. I tried so hard for that not to happen, but I couldn't control myself.

"Mom, what's wrong?" said Emilie, as she jumped from her chair to my side. Reese also got up and put her arms around me. "Mom, what is it?"

"We have to talk. There's something that was discovered that I have to tell you about."

"Tell us? Tell us what?" asked Reese.

"Let's go in the family room," I said, as we walked in together with our arms around one other. We all sat down. "Kristee Adams, and I know this is going to sound unbelievable, tried to assume my identity to take out money that was in a secret account that Dad had set up in Turks."

"What?" said Emilie, her eyes wide open.

"Why was there money in a secret account?" asked Reese.

"And why did Kristee know about it and not you?" added Emilie.

"I don't know, and I don't know why the account was set up or how Kristee knew about it. I'm as shocked as you are about it."

"So, she knew about this money somehow, and then she tried to go and get it after Dad died," said Reese.

"Yes."

"How much money is it?" asked Emilie.

"Eight million dollars."

"Geez!" Reese said, as she sat back and looked up to the ceiling. "So Kristee, acting like you, tried to get the money that you would have gotten as a widow? Correct? Because when you're married, everything belongs to each other even if your spouse's name isn't on it."

"Well, almost. My name was on the account, so she was trying to act like me as an account holder."

"How could your name be on the account when you didn't know about it?" asked Reese.

"Well, that's what is really puzzling. The president of First

Caribbean Bank told me that each year for eight years, a million-dollar check was written out to me from the company and placed into the account by Dad."

"That makes no sense," said Emilie. "There has to be more to all of this. This banker person—how did you find this out from him?"

"When I went to Turks to close up the house when it was going to be sold, he came over to express his condolences about Dad's death. I asked him how he knew Dad had died, and he said that our real estate agent had told him. I thanked him for stopping by, but I also told him that I was really surprised that he would come by since the only interaction we had had with him was when we first bought the house. I had never actually met him. And then he told me that I had all this money in the joint account with Dad. I almost fainted. That's why I stopped the sale—since I had all this money I didn't know about."

"This is really all too much," said Emilie. "And how did the bank president know that Kristee tried to get the money and it wasn't you just saying that you wanted to take out the money, which is rightfully yours?"

"Okay, this is really going to be hard for you to understand, but please hear me out. Leon, Leon Abramson, that is, the president of the bank, is a widower. He used to live in London, and sadly, his wife and son were killed in a car accident by a drunk driver. When I went over to his office the day after he told me about the money to look at the file, I asked him to dinner, and we started seeing one another."

"When you say 'seeing one another,' what do you mean?" asked Emilie, indignantly.

"I mean we started to spend time together. I know it sounds crazy."

"Mom, are you in a sexual relationship with this Leon?" Reese got right to the point.

Before I could answer, Emilie asked, "Mom, do you really expect us to believe all this? Dad just died, and you're having sex with a stranger!" At that, she stood up. "This is just not possible. Reese, come with me. I think we need to go to Kristee's house and talk to her about all of this." Reese got up and followed her into the kitchen.

"You can't do that." I said. "She's in jail in Turks and Caicos." They turned and walked back into the family room.

"She's in jail?" questioned Emilie. "For real?"

"Leon got a call at the bank from a woman saying she was Clair Bondi and wanted to come in and take out the money."

"And of course, he knew it wasn't you because the two of you were having sex," said Reese.

"Come on, Reese, this is hard enough. Don't make it worse. Leon had to alert the authorities, and they arrested her in his office."

"This is like a movie or a nightmare," said Reese, sitting back down on the sofa.

"I can't believe this was all going on, and you never told us," said Emilie.

"I just found out yesterday that it was Kristee. But unfortunately, there's more."

"More? What more could there possibly be than what you already told us? Dad had an employee who stole from him. That's the bottom line."

"I feel I should tell you everything because I want to be totally honest with you. Dad had two affairs that I know about—one eight years ago with our jeweler and one just recently with a consultant for the company."

"Oh, man, no, no," said Reese.

"And did you do anything about this or try to stop it?" asked

Emilie, throwing her arms up in the air.

"Well, I did the first time, but I didn't have time to try and do anything the second time because it just happened, or at least I just found out about it." I didn't want to tell them that I was planning on getting a divorce.

"And how did you find out about the second one?" asked Reese.

"I hired a detective, and he caught them."

"All right, enough," said Emilie. "I've heard enough. I'm going upstairs."

"Me, too," said Reese.

Chapter 22

It was evident from our conversation that the girls, like me, didn't think anything was going on sexually between Vince and Kristee. I would just have to wait until Kristee's trial and see what would come out. I knew the money thing was difficult for them to hear and understand, but the realization that I was seeing another man was worse.

I had no sooner turned out the lights downstairs and walked up to my bedroom than the girls came into my room. Their eyes were red, and their faces were puffy. Reese asked, "Mom, what happened between you and Dad? I mean, before all of this happened with Dad's death and now all this stuff about Kristee. When did it all start—the cheating, I mean?" I could see it was difficult for her to get out the words.

Before I could answer, Emilie said, "You never acted like anything was wrong."

"There were issues, but I didn't say anything. Dad had changed over the last few years. He was distant, I guess, is the best way to explain it. I tried my best to see what was wrong because I loved your father. You know that. He was everything to me. Just like the two of you. I finally hired the detective and found out about the affair right before we were supposed to go to Turks and Caicos. I didn't say anything since I didn't see any other alternative. I hadn't had a real husband-wife relationship with your father for quite some time." I couldn't bring myself to just come out and say we weren't having sex, so it sounded awkward. "I was going to deal with it all after the trip, and then Dad was killed."

"I can't believe you hired a detective," said Emilie.

"I had to see it for myself. But when Dad died, my goal was never to have you girls find out about their relationship. What would be the reason? You had been through enough after losing Dad. You didn't need to deal with this, too."

And then, surprisingly, Reese said, taking my hand, "Mom, what about what you have been through?" Reese was suddenly sounding like Leon.

I tried to hold it all together and said, "I used to think I just wanted to protect the two of you, but I think the reality of the situation is that I didn't want to have to face it myself—the affair, that is."

Reese said, "Mom, Emilie and I are here to support you. Even though this is horrible, and it sucks every way around, we are here for you. "

I was so relieved to hear Reese speak those words. "Thank you, honey."

"You don't have to thank us. We're all in this together." I could only imagine her as a doctor telling someone that their loved one had died. She would be comforting and reassuring, even at a very sad moment.

"And what about this banker? I forget his name," asked Emilie.

"Leon. Leon Abramson. He's wonderful. I never thought I

would be able to care for someone like I do for Leon. It all happened so quickly, I realize. I'm sure you're worried that he might not be as great as I'm making him out to be, but he really is."

The girls looked at one another and then back to me.

"Mom, I hope you can understand what a shock all this is, but we're trying to take it all in," said Emilie. She stood up, walked over to the window, opened the shutter, letting in the darkness of night, and then closed it again. "We want you to be happy, and if Leon makes you happy, well then, we're in. But we are concerned. You're very vulnerable right now. Do you understand that?"

"I do."

"I hope to meet him someday," said Reese.

"Me, too," said Emilie.

I stared at both of them and didn't say anything, but I must have had a strange look on my face because together they both said, "What?" I was amazed how many times this type of thing happened, maybe because they were twins.

"Well... Leon is here, actually. Not here, like in the house, but nearby. He wanted to be here for support."

"He's here?" asked Emilie, with surprise.

"Yes, at the Marriott."

"Wow, that's amazing... I guess," said Reese, apprehensively. "Are there any other shockers we need to get out in the open?"

"God, no, thank goodness," I said. I could feel the tension in my face ease up a bit. "That's it. Everything is out now."

"Kristee Adams. I still can't believe it. She was so nice to us," said Reese, getting up from the sofa.

"It's so hard to believe. What will happen to her now?" asked Emilie.

"We'll have to see what the court does in Turks. It's up to them. But there will be a trial here in Philadelphia for the shooter since he's pleading not guilty. That's why Leon wanted to come.

He felt it was too much for me to deal with, and I know he would be thrilled to meet you both." I was so hoping they would be happy about that, too, but it appeared they needed a bit more time, understandably.

"Yes, of course, we'll meet him," said Reese. "How long will he be here?"

"A week."

"Okay. We just wanted to come in and tell you that we support you, and we love you."

"Thanks, girls. Love you, too."

I was exhausted but wanted to send Leon a quick text that everything was okay with the girls. As I looked at my phone, I saw a text from Jane. *Need to meet with you on Monday. Are you free?* I wrote back that I was and wondered how she had come up with something so quickly. I was curious and wanted to know. I felt the power to move forward now that the girls knew everything.

I went into the bathroom and took off my makeup, even though I didn't feel like it, brushed my teeth, and got into a pair of pajamas. The slip I had worn with Leon the night before lay on my dressing table in my closet. It was a nice reminder of being with him.

As eager as I was to go to sleep, I wasn't able to. I got into bed, but tossed and turned. I was too keyed up to sleep. An hour passed, and I was still up. Everything was racing in my head. I kept thinking of Vince. For some reason, I got to thinking about the tapes that Steve Madison had given me when he was following Vince. He had given me two tapes, but I'd only watched the one—not the other "B-roll," as he called it. After seeing what I needed to know about Vince and Catherine's affair, I didn't bother to watch it. But suddenly I was curious about what was on it.

I decided to get the box of stuff I had stashed in my closet that was from the detective. He had given me a complete, typed narrative about the followings as well as the tapes. I closed my bedroom door, even though I knew the girls were fast asleep and that they wouldn't hear me in the other wing of the house.

I propped up my pillows, put on my glasses, and put in the DVD. I didn't want to admit this to myself, but I think I just wanted to see Vince on the tape. I had no idea if he would be on it since it was just video of people going in and out of the office. Vince was on the tape. It showed him leaving the office as the detectives started to follow him downtown when he met Catherine at the Four Seasons.

But right after Vince left, a car pulled up—a navy blue Mustang with vanity plates that said TC100. The TC immediately made me think of Turks and Caicos, so I was drawn to it. No sooner had the car arrived with a man at the wheel than Kristee came out of the office, and he got out of the car. They were smiling at one another, and Kristee handed him an envelope. He took it, opened it, and took out what appeared to be a check. He put it back into the envelope, and they started laughing. Then he got back in his car and drove off.

I felt like I was becoming paranoid and suspicious of everything. Whatever had taken place, I knew I needed to tell Captain Martin about it, and I planned on doing it first thing in the morning, which wasn't that far away.

June 1, 2012
Philadelphia Police Department—Detective Division
One Market Square
Philadelphia, PA

"What do you have for me, Edwards?"

"Clair Bondi called this morning very upset."

"I can certainly understand with all that she's going through," said Captain Martin.

"She wanted to talk to you, but I handled it."

"Whenever she calls, feel free to put the call through to me."

"I just came from her house and picked up this DVD she wants us to check out. It's from the detective when she had her husband followed right before he was shot. Some B-roll from in front of his office building. Seems there's this guy on it who pulls up in his car, and Kristee Adams, Vince's office assistant, comes out and hands him a check. Could be nothing, I suppose, but I think we should check it out."

"Most definitely."

"Okay. I'll let you know what I find out."

Chapter 23

Although I was concerned about the revelation of Kristee with the unknown man and the envelope, I knew I had to put it out of my mind. The tape was now in the hands of Captain Martin, and I would just have to wait and see what he thought. I was relieved that Detective Edwards came right over and picked it up.

The girls slept in, and I wanted to talk to them about meeting Leon when they got up. It felt great to have them home. The house felt alive, even though they were still asleep. When they got up around eleven, I came in at the side door from a walk while they were having breakfast. They had made smoothies—kale, avocado, honey, and banana.

"Good morning. Wow, this looks great," I said, picking up one of the glasses and admiring the creamy smoothie.

"It's for you, and yes, we put your precious flax seeds in," said Emilie, with a supercilious look.

I wanted to see if they would be up for Leon coming over for a visit, even though I felt anxious bringing it up. "Hey, guys, listen, how about if we have Leon over for a casual dinner tonight? He would very much like to meet you both."

"Well," said Emilie, looking at Reese, "we're going over to see Nan and Pop this afternoon, and I don't know how long we'll be."

Reese, luckily, saved the moment. "We'll be back in time. Sounds good. Say seven?"

"Great. I'll tell Leon."

I decided to keep things simple—just chicken fried rice, salad, and wine. The day went quickly, and before I knew it, Leon was at the side door. I kept telling myself to relax. I didn't want to greet him my usual way, where I couldn't get to him fast enough and held onto him until I had to let go.

"Hi," I said, softly, while the girls were in the family room. "I'm crazy to see you—just think I need to cool it a bit with my welcome."

He smiled. Of course he looked great—dark jeans, a blue shirt, and a Polo black vest. He had a bouquet of white hydrangeas wrapped in clear paper with a lime green ribbon.

The girls heard him come in and walked into the kitchen.

"Girls, Leon's here."

It was an awkward moment as we all stood there. "Hi, girls," he said. "It's a pleasure to meet you. My deepest condolences."

"Thank you," said Reese, returning his extended hand.

"A pleasure to meet you," added Emilie.

I put the flowers in a vase and opened a bottle of Flowers Pinot Noir. The girls took Leon into the family room, where I had a cheese board on the cocktail table. They were gracious, but I knew it was difficult for them. They had never seen me with a man other than their father.

"So now, which of you is the soon-to-be attorney?"

"That would be me, Emilie."

"Congrats, so you have one more year? Correct?"

"It took me four, or it will have taken me four, I should say, to finish my three-year law degree."

"Oh," said Leon.

I could see he wasn't sure what to say. Emilie was messing with him a bit. "Emilie had a biking accident at the beginning of her second year," I said. "Broke her elbow and had to have it totally reconstructed, so she had to delay a year with healing and physical therapy."

"So now," added Reese, "we'll graduate at the same time."

"Terrific. I hope everything is good with the arm now."

"All good." Emilie moved her elbow, turning it all different ways.

"And, Reese, have you chosen what type of doctor you would like to be?"

"Brain surgeon," kidded Emilie.

"So I can operate on you, right?" Reese joked back. "I've always wanted to help people in rehab, so I might concentrate on stroke recovery. I'm pretty sure that will be it."

"That's very admirable."

And then out of the blue, Emilie really shocked me. "Leon, I'm so sorry for the loss of your wife and son. Mom told us about that. I'm really sorry." I could see that Emilie really meant those kind words.

"Yes," added Reese.

"Thank you."

I excused myself and went into the kitchen. I could hear the girls talking with Leon about his charity work in Haiti. The good, warm, interesting conversation continued at the table, and it went very well. The girls had plans to go to a movie with some friends, so Leon and I had the rest of the evening to ourselves. Our conversation continued in a serious manner.

"Clair, this is a delicate time for you, and as much as I want to be here to support you, I think you need this time with your daughters. They are very nice girls—young women—but it's the three of you right now. There will be time for us later."

I had been thinking the same thing, so it was a relief that he had felt that way. "I agree with you, Leon."

He put his arms around me as we stood by the kitchen sink. He kissed me tenderly and said, "I love you, Clair Bondi."

It was sad when he left that evening, but I knew it was right. I had no idea when I would see him again, but I had to just see how things played out. I went to bed, but I heard the girls come in around ten.

On Sunday afternoon, I got a text from Leon saying he was taking off and that he would text me when he got back to Turks. Jane also texted, asking if 10:00 a.m. was too early to meet on Monday. She wanted to know if it would be easier to meet at my home, rather than Vince's office. I didn't want to meet at either place, so we decided to meet at her office in Bala Cynwyd, about twenty minutes from my house.

———————————

Monday came quickly, and I was eager to get on with things. I had no idea what Jane had come up with, but I was anxious to find out.

"Hi, Clair, how are you?"

"Okay, thanks."

"All right." I could see she was eager to get right down to business. "I didn't have a chance to go through everything, but there are a few things that stood out that I wanted to bring to your attention."

"Okay."

"So, are you aware of an apartment that Vince had rented

through the company?"

"No," I said.

"Well, there is an apartment in New Hope—628 Riverview Terrace, to be exact."

"I never heard of it."

"You might want to talk to Jim Stone about it and see why it was rented. The lease has been in place for the last five years at a monthly rate of four thousand a month."

"Must be a nice place."

"Let me just say, no one rents a property for investment."

"So what are you saying? That maybe it was his place that he used for his mistress and used company money to pay for it?"

"I'm just giving you the facts."

I was trying my best not to act emotional, but I was not happy to hear of this.

"Okay, so next, I want to ask you about a file marked *200 Leber Hill.* Does that address ring a bell? Is it one of your development pieces?"

"No."

"Well, that house is owned by Kristee Adams and has over $100,000 in renovations done by a Doug Grotto."

We stared at each other and didn't say anything.

"We both know who Kristee Adams is, so tell me who Doug Grotto is," she said, breaking the silence.

"Doug Grotto is a close friend of Vince's, or I should say, was a great friend of Vince's. He's a builder, and he's done lots of things for us to our Villanova home."

"Well, he did things for Kristee Adams, and the checks were paid by the steel business. The file also has receipts for some antiques, plantation shutters, and some furniture."

"Unbelievable." I was beginning to see that there was more to the Vince/Kristee business relationship, and Jane knew I was seeing it, too.

"Okay. We're getting through. Next, there are three checks made payable to Kristee Adams for $40,000 each, separated by two-week intervals, two months before she purchased her home."

"How did you find out it was before she purchased her home?"

"I looked up the settlement date."

"Maybe the down payment?" I asked.

"Many times people break up checks over fifty thousand so not to draw attention to larger checks. Could create some suspicion. It's usually with cash transactions, but people still do it with checks, as well." She got right to the next question before I could react to the information. "And then there are some purchases you made in Italy, for jewelry, clothing, etcetera. I assume the two of you took a trip to Italy—Taormina? Was that with you?"

"Yes, that was with me, but I didn't buy any jewelry, nor did Vince buy any for me."

"Well, there was a bracelet and a ring bought at a store in Taormina."

"Wasn't for me."

"I know this is a lot. I see this type of thing more often that I would like." She paused for a moment and then continued. "The company had paid for all these things I have mentioned. You really need to talk to Jim Stone about this."

"I plan to."

"And while you're asking, there is one more thing that is raising a red flag. As I looked over some business transactions, and there certainly are legitimate business transactions, I found one written the day your husband was murdered. It's a check for $500,000 made out to CR Consulting."

"Oh, I know what that has to be—Catherine Rogers, his business consultant."

"Clair, did Vince share with you what he was doing with the

business?"

"Vince was his own guy—he didn't share things with Jim, either. I know that. Jim handled the operational side, but it was all Vince—he made all the decisions and it was his baby, so he did things his way. I, on the other hand, had no voice whatsoever."

"Okay. I understand. But who wrote out the checks?"

"I would think Vince and Jim, but I don't know for sure."

"You need to have a frank conversation with Jim. You don't think there could be any funny business going on with him and Kristee regarding the books, do you?"

"God, I don't know. When Jim said he would keep everything going, I never thought that maybe he shouldn't be the person doing all of that."

"Well, let me know what you find out. I'll be eager to hear."

"Okay. I'll get on it. Thanks so much."

As crazy and as difficult as it was to hear what all the discoveries were, I couldn't believe what Jane had found. I was relieved that I had hired her. Now I had to have a very difficult talk with Jim. I called him from the car and asked if we could meet. Luckily, he said to come right over if I wanted to, so I did. I wasn't going to mention the money for the jewelry, but I needed to ask about the apartment and the check to CR Consulting, as well as the checks to Kristee, since those were all paid by the business.

Jim was on the phone when I arrived, but he got off quickly. "Hi, Clair," he said as he hung up and offered me a seat in his office. I could see Vince's office right down the hallway, which felt strange. I had never actually been in Jim's office. He closed the door, even though no one else was there. "How are you? And your daughters?"

"I'm hanging in, Jim, and so are they." I hated that expression, but for some reason it just came out. "I have a few things I need to discuss."

"Okay, sure."

"The apartment in New Hope," I started to say, but then he jumped in and said, "Oh, yes, perfect timing. I just got a letter that the lease is up in two months, and I wanted to ask you if you wanted to renew it for another year. I'd be happy to handle that for you, but I didn't know how you would feel going there under the circumstances."

"What exactly do you mean?" I asked.

"Well, now that Vince has passed away. I didn't know if you wanted to use it anymore. I can certainly understand if you don't."

"Jim, I didn't even know about the apartment until this morning when I met with an accountant." I didn't want to use the word forensic, since he might think that I was fishing around for things, even though I was.

"What? I don't understand."

"Look, Jim. It's obvious that Vince and Kristee used the apartment and that I was never supposed to know about it."

"I can't answer to that."

He really ticked me off. "Jim, you can't answer to that? Well, guess what, you're going to have to. Let's not play games. I'm sure that you knew that he and Kristee used the place."

"Clair, I didn't know that. It was set up as a corporate apartment, but I assumed that you and Vince used it mostly."

"Well, you assumed incorrectly. I have never been there, and I don't want to have it any longer. Don't renew the lease. Just stop it. I don't care what he or she may have there. I don't really care."

"Whatever you wish, Clair."

"Remember, Jim, you and I are both owners of this company, too." I could hear Jane's words cheering me on in my head. "And money that went to that apartment came from money that belongs to us."

"Yes. That's correct. I hope you realize that I had nothing to do with what the money was spent on. Whatever Vince did with the money was all his decision. I was happy to have a minority ownership, which gave my family a nice life. I didn't ask any questions."

"Well, maybe we both should have. At any rate, there were several checks written to Kristee that shouldn't have been. I'm not going to go into all the details, but Vince gave her money from the company, whether you knew or didn't know about it."

"As I said, I did not know."

It was clear that Jim was not going to tell me whether he knew about things or not, but I felt I had to ask about the one check written to CR Consulting.

"Jim, you surely must have been aware of CR Consulting— Catherine Rogers."

"Yes, I was."

"Were you aware that on the day Vince was fatally shot there was a check written out to CR Consulting?"

"No, I was not."

"So, the only person who could have written that check was Vince, correct? Or did you have the capacity to write checks, as well?"

"I have the capacity to write checks, but I never wrote a really important check—only those under $500,000, that is. Vince wrote out checks for monies over that amount. That was the paradigm we had set up."

I had no idea if Jim was lying. I realized at that moment that I had to get rid of him. For now, I would have him continue to run things, but I would have to know what was going on. "From here on in, Jim, I need to see every check that is written and compare it to the bank statement each month. You okay with that?"

"Yes. That's fine."

"Okay, Jim, talk soon. Let me know if anything comes up. Oh, one more thing: how long did Kristee work for Vince?"

"Six years this month."

"Okay, thanks."

"Sure, Clair." At that, I left the office not sure if anything was really straightened out.

———————————

June 8, 2012
Philadelphia Police Department—Detective Division
One Market Square
Philadelphia, PA

"Hey, Captain. I just got the information about the guy with the envelope and Mrs. Bondi, or I should say, Kristee Adams."

"What did you find?"

"Well, the tape had a good look at the vehicle the guy was driving, so I ran a report on his plates, TC100. It's owned by a Tom Coleada of Bridgeport. He has a record—he served time for white-collar crime and identity theft.

"Seems he got involved for a while with the Mafia guys back in the '80s who all went to that condo in Ocean City, New Jersey. There's news footage of the police investigating them all. Seems he ran a front for them, working their investments, but they weren't really investments, if you get my drift. He's the same guy. He's actually a real financial guy, degrees and certifications and all, but seems he got hooked up with some bad eggs. I don't see him employed anywhere, but I have an address for him. This could be big."

"I think you're right, Edwards. We owe Mr. Coleada a visit. I want to talk to Mrs. Bondi first and let her know what we found."

"I'd be happy to call her and report back," said Detective Edwards.

"Thanks, but I'll handle it."

Chapter 24

I started thinking about Jim, and the more I thought about him, the more frightened I was that he could have been ripping the company off for years. It was he who controlled the day-to-day. I knew for a fact that Vince didn't get caught up in the details. He made the deals, and I knew that he left the rest up to Jim. I needed to talk with Jane about it and get her thoughts. I was sure she'd had experience with this type of thing. I tried to get her, but she didn't pick up. I left her a message that I had some information for her.

No sooner had I gotten off that call than I got the call I had been waiting for. "Hello, Mrs. Bondi. How are you?"

"Fine, thanks, Captain Martin. Did you find out anything?"

"Interesting enough, yes, we did. We ran a trace on the tags of the car in the tape, and it belongs to a convicted felon who did some white-collar crime—identity thief. He got mixed up with a Philadelphia Mafia group years ago, so something could be up with him and Kristee. At the very least, we need to bring him in for questioning."

"Oh my God. What do you think the two of them could have done together?"

"I couldn't tell you at this point, but we'll find out."

"I'm curious as to who this person is. What's his name? Where does he live?"

"His name is Tom Coleada, and he lives in Bridgeport."

"Do you think Vince was involved with the mob?"

"We don't know yet, Clair. Let me do my work, and we'll figure it out."

"Okay. But he could have been in on the Mafia connection, too. I remember when Reese was in high school, she came home crying one day because some kids said that Vince was in the Mafia. Maybe it was true. And if it was, I might have to pay the government a lot of money from the company."

"Let's not get ahead of ourselves. We'll fit all the pieces together and get to the bottom of all of this. I need to start with Tom Coleada."

I couldn't believe it. That could be the only answer to all of this—the mob. And obviously, Vince was killed because of it. And that also explained the money in the secret account in Turks. Vince needed to hide some money from the mob, and Kristee was in on it. They probably needed a straight man to run the business, too, at least for the sake of the IRS, and that could have been Jim. My head was spinning.

An entire week had passed, and I said nothing to anyone about the new developments. I talked with Leon, but I didn't mention anything about the case. I kept the conversation light. We told each other we missed one another, which was certainly true. I longed to see him, touch him, and have him by my side. The girls spent their time catching up with friends.

And then I got the call from Captain Martin. He wanted me to come down to the station. It must have been important, since he asked me to bring someone with me, but I decided to go alone. When I got there, both Captain Martin and Detective Edwards were waiting for me. The office was a dismal space, gray everything—chairs, desks, walls. A small photo of Frank Rizzo, the late police commissioner and mayor, hung on the wall.

"Clair, thanks for coming. Please sit down," said Captain Martin. He was in street clothes—a pair of gray trousers and a gray shirt with a black belt—so he looked very different from when I had seen him previously. He sat down in his desk chair and asked, "How are you doing?" as he placed a file, obviously mine, in front of him. Detective Edwards was standing, leaning on the side of the doorframe after she closed the door to his office.

"Okay," I said. I could feel something was about to happen, and it wouldn't be good. Maybe something really bad. I looked at Captain Martin and then back at Detective Edwards, and she looked at him with a look suggesting that he begin telling me something I was going to be shocked to hear.

"Well, we have some important developments. We brought in Tom Coleada and asked him if he knew Kristee Adams. He said that he and Kristee were in business together running an escort service, but he never wanted his wife to know about it because she would disapprove.

"I asked more about the business—how they ran it, who did what, etc. Not important to go into all of that at this juncture. He said he had put up money initially for their business and that Kristee had to pay him back some money, so that was the reason for the check she had given him. He said it was from Kristee's personal account, and it was for $1,000.

"After that meeting, we let him go, and we kept a detective on him. There was nothing out of the ordinary. He basically stayed in his house and occasionally went out to a local diner with his wife. He didn't leave his house during the day, but the wife went to her job as a teller at a nearby bank. Obviously, he wasn't working, or if he was, he was doing it from home."

"Mrs. Bondi," said Detective Edwards, as she walked over to the desk and sat in the chair next to me, "there was something in my gut that didn't feel right, or I should say, that was telling me to take a second look at the surveillance tape that we had from the 7-Eleven after I had looked at your tape from the detective. If you remember, we had gotten it from the store when we had interviewed the clerk there."

"Yes, I remember. You mentioned that Vince had gone in there to buy black licorice when he stopped on his way home from tennis that night."

"Yes, that's correct," she said. "After reviewing that tape, I rewatched the detective tape."

"Okay." I wasn't sure where she was going with all of this, but I continued to listen.

"When I had initially looked at that tape, my focus was on the license plate to see who owned the car and if the owner had a record of any sort. And of course, we know now that Tom Coleada has a record."

"Yes."

"Okay. But what I hadn't done at that initial viewing was focus on the physical components of the man receiving the envelope, Tom Coleada. I hadn't looked at his movements, etcetera. When I focused in on his movements the second time I watched the tape, I noticed that he constantly rubbed his neck, behind his right ear, only that ear. He did it several times, or I should say, enough times that it caught my attention.

"I then went back to the 7-Eleven surveillance tape and focused on the police officer who happened to be in the 7-Eleven the same time that Vince was. There were other people in the 7-Eleven, as well, and they were all going about their business of shopping and paying for what they bought. There didn't appear to be anything out of the ordinary when we first watched the tape. When I re-watched the tape, I noticed the same neck rubbing behind the right ear of the police officer that Tom Coleada had done on the detective tape. When I thought it could possibly be the same person, I had the images run through our facial recognition software and received feedback that it was highly likely." At that, she leaned back in her chair as if to give me time to take it all in.

"Oh, my God," I said.

"You want to take it from here, Captain?" she asked.

He sat up in his chair a bit straighter. "We brought Tom Coleada back in for questioning. We told him we had tapes and information that would prove his guilt for the murder of Vincent Bondi. We read him his rights, he obtained a lawyer, and we then met with the two of them. We told him we have him on tape receiving a check from Kristee and on tape at the 7-Eleven impersonating a police officer. He and his lawyer talked after that, obviously with a discussion about a possible life in prison for a first-degree murder verdict, and his lawyer requested a meeting with the prosecutor, Diana Silver."

I must have had a horrified look my face because Detective Martin asked, "Are you still with me, Clair? I know this is a lot to follow."

"Yes."

"After the meeting with the prosecutor and the knowledge that Kristee is also involved with the crime, Tom's lawyer explained the evidence they had on him and suggested a plea bargain, where he admitted to the murder of Vince in exchange for a lesser sentence with an explanation of Kristee's involvement, as well as any other information about the crime. The last one is most important to Prosecutor Silver because her goal is to prove that Kristee arranged for the murder. She's seen too many cases where a jury comes back with an innocent verdict citing circumstantial evidence, and the person walks. She doesn't want that to happen."

I was numb. "Why in God's name would Kristee have someone she supposedly loved killed?" I asked. "And how could she think to do such a thing for whatever reason she did?"

"Well," said Captain Martin, "we asked Tom Coleada if he knew why she wanted him killed. I realize this is going to be painful to hear, but he told us that Vince told her that he was going to divorce you and marry her and then move to Turks and Caicos. She believed that was never going to happen, so she felt that she was going to get the $8 million."

Oh, my God. I broke down.

Captain Martin tried to console me. "We will bring her to justice for all of this. Kristee is being extradited to Philadelphia as we speak for arranging the shooting of your husband. She is being brought back by US marshals. We have the full cooperation of the Turks and Caicos police and customs departments. And we will certainly talk to her when she gets here."

Well, there it was. The story was perfect for a movie. Only it wasn't. It was my life, and I hated it. Vince's entanglements had wreaked havoc on my life and the lives of my daughters. "Why in God's name would Kristee have someone she supposedly loved killed?" It was difficult to get out those words, but that was the first thing that came to my mind. "How could she think to do such a thing for whatever reason she did it? How could she kill a person? Didn't she think she would get caught?"

"Well," said Captain Martin, "I assure you we will find all that out. "

"Do you think you will be able to get her to confess?" I asked, as I looked to both of them.

"That's our goal. If we can, we won't have to go to trial, and that will be good for everyone," he said, assuredly.

And suddenly, all I could think of was the young man being falsely held. "What about the man accused? Can he be let go now?"

"We'll be working on that."

"Oh, God, this is going to be a nightmare. I don't know how you figured all this out. It's really incredible. And Detective Edwards, I can't believe you picked up on the hand movement of Tom Coleada."

She replied, "Luckily, it was that hand movement that brought me to his face."

"Thank you both so much."

Captain Martin replied, "We're just doing our jobs. We're sorry you had to go through all of this, not to mention the loss to your family."

They walked me to the door, and I walked out of the station with the resolve that there was no time for pity, sadness, or tears. The time had come for me to draw strength from every depth of my body and soul to see all this through.

Chapter 25

As I was walking to the parking garage from the police station to get my car, my phone buzzed. It was Leon. It amazed me how he always knew when I needed him the most, just like he did when I saw him at my side door after the customs agents came to see me.

"Hi, Leon," I said, trying to sound like I was okay when I really wasn't.

"Are you okay, Clair? Where are you?"

"I just left the police station. Not only did Kristee try to get the money, she had Vince killed, not to mention their affair. It was the man Tom Coleada on my detective's tape—TC100. I watched it the other night and saw Kristee handing him a check. Too complicated to explain all right now, but they got a plea bargain for his admitting that he killed Vince. I'll fill you in later. She's an animal as far as I'm concerned. How am I supposed to explain this to the girls? They're never going to be able to deal with this."

"Yes, they will, Clair. They will have to. It's really all over now."

"Yes, it is."

"Clair, are you sure you're okay to drive home?"

And then it suddenly, quite expectantly, became clear to me what I wanted to do. "Leon, it could be a few weeks until Kristee gets back here and the prosecutor and her lawyer all talk and see what happens. The girls and I will be coming to Turks while they are off. We are only a three-hour flight away for when we need to come back."

"Are you sure they'll be okay with that?"

"They'll have to be. I'm not going to sit around here day after day waiting for this to all be over. I'm going to spend it in the most beautiful place I know—Turks."

"Gosh, Clair, of course I think that's great. It's wonderful. I'm thrilled."

"I'm living my life. And, I want to be with you. You're the most wonderful thing that has happened to me."

"I feel the same way, Clair. You know that."

"Yes, I do. I love you, Leon."

"I love you, too, Clair."

When I got home, I told the girls everything. They were shocked and horrified like I was, but I think they were relieved to know my plan of going to Turks. We all agreed that we were going to get through this together. We had faced the worst, and now we just had to see justice served.

Emilie was helpful with filling me in on how the legal process would proceed, but I didn't need to know every detail. The lawyers could do all of that. Kristee had Vince killed. End of story. Nothing else really mattered—not the affair, not the money she tried to take out. I felt Buddhist-like, rising above all that I needed to in order to get to a better place. It seemed incredible. One day you're going along, and suddenly the whole world falls apart. I felt like Nick Carraway in *The Great Gatsby*: "The loneliest moment in someone's life is when they are watching their whole world fall apart, and all they can do is stare blankly."

When I got home, the girls went out for dinner, but I couldn't think about eating. I collapsed onto my bed and woke up at midnight. I checked on the girls, and they were fast asleep. They had left a note outside my door that said they didn't have the heart to wake me after the day we all had.

I checked my phone and saw that Leon had called. He was a night owl and a big Stephen Colbert fan, so I knew he didn't go to bed until after the show. I picked up my phone and called him.

"How did the girls take everything, and more, importantly, how are you?"

"We're pretty good, all things considered."

"Terrific."

"And, best news yet, the girls want to come to Turks."

"Great. When can I expect you?"

"I'll look at flights tomorrow, so maybe a day or two after that."

"I want to send a plane for you. Just tell me when, and I'll have it there. It will be great to have you here, along with the girls."

"Oh my gosh, are you sure?"

"Yes. You've all been through so much. A relaxing flight down will be much better than flying commercial."

"Okay, I'll take you up on that. Thank you so much. Leon, I want to do something."

"And what is that?" he asked.

"Remember I told you about the young woman at my university who told me that she had given up her daughter for adoption?"

"Yes, I do. I remember you were very taken with her."

"Right. I want to see if you can help us find her daughter."

"Of course. I just need some information from her. Would it be okay for me to talk with her?"

"That would be terrific. And, Leon, I want to go to Haiti with you and the girls. I want to see what you do there."

"Really?"

"Yes. Any volunteer work I have ever done has just entailed writing a check. I want to do more. I want to help in some way."

"You seem to be taking on a lot—helping Ursula and wanting to go to Haiti."

"I need to. I want to. My life has to have more meaning and purpose. It just can't be about making money."

"Okay, then. All those things can be worked out."

I loved his enthusiasm. I often heard of people who are in love say they are a better person because of the other. I felt that way with Leon.

"Hey," he said, changing the conversation. "Stephen Colbert has on Tina Fey. Are you watching?"

"I will be," I said with a smile. I always thought it was interesting that we instinctively smile even when no one is around to see it. "I'll let you go. Talk to you tomorrow. Good night."

And so it was. A great man was in my life, and despite what was happening, it felt good. I bet Nick Carraway would have loved Leon.

Chapter 26

I was relieved that both Captain Martin and Detective Edwards gave me the green light to go to Turks. And I was surprised that Leon was able to locate Ursula's daughter through an agency in just four days.

Her name was Joanne Motley. The sixteen year old lived in Chestnut Hill with her parents, Louis K. Motley, a Philadelphia judge, and her mother, Mavis Motley, a professor at the University of Pennsylvania. Ursula lived only a few miles from the Motleys, but their lives were as different as night and day. The boarded-up homes of Ursula's North Philadelphia neighborhood were in stark contrast to the charming stone houses of fashionable Chestnut Hill.

The agency was able to contact the family, and the Motleys couldn't have been more wonderful. They told the social worker they had prepared their daughter for the possibility of this day and told her that when she turned eighteen, if her birth mother hadn't sought her out before that time, she would be free to try to find her.

Ursula was shocked beyond belief. We had a very tearful phone conversation, and she asked me if I would go with her when they meet. I had to go. I couldn't imagine seeing my daughters at sixteen for the first time.

Ursula had never gotten to see her daughter when she gave birth. The child was taken away before she had a chance to hold her, and she was left in her hospital room with her grandmother. She never got to know that extraordinary surreal experience of when your baby is placed in your arms.

When I had the twins, Vince got to cut their umbilical cords. He was so nervous. He so wanted to do it right. I remember the doctor telling him that it wasn't difficult. I loved that moment. I don't think there could be a tighter bond between a husband and wife than that moment of the birth of their child. What could be better than the beginning of life? Vince held one of the girls, and I held the other. I can't remember whether I held Emilie or Reese, since we hadn't named them yet at that moment. But I will never forget seeing their little bodies and their tiny, tiny hands and feet. We were so young, but we loved our family.

I didn't want Ursula to go through the experience herself. I had an idea. "Girls," I said one night at dinner, "how would you feel if Ursula stayed with us before she meets Joanne? She could come over after her workday at Campbell Soup. I don't want her to face all of this alone."

"Oh, of course," said Reese.

"I agree!" said Emilie.

"Let's get her on the phone," I said.

She answered right away with a soft hello.

"Ursula, how about a little change of scenery?" I asked.

"Put her on speaker," said Reese, wiping tomato sauce from her mouth.

"The girls are here, Ursula, and we want to ask you to come and stay with us."

"We're all here for a time before we go to Turks, so we want you here, too," said Emilie. "It will be fun."

Ursula was a bit hesitant, but then agreed when we all excitingly said in unison, "Come!"

"Okay! I'll come over tomorrow night after work," she said, as we bombarded her with our excitement.

I knew having Ursula with us would be a benefit to her, but also to me. It would take my mind off things, although I was eager to get to Turks. Leon understood and was happy with what we had planned, even if it meant delaying our arrival.

The girls suggested that Ursula take something the day she went—something for the Motleys and something for Joanne. In the end, we all agreed that maybe a bouquet of flowers would be best. She didn't want to come on too strong, yet she wanted to bring a gift. She also put a lot of thought into what she would wear—she didn't want to look too dressed up, yet not too casual.

When that Saturday morning came for the visit, it was a beautiful day in late June. Pulling up to their three-story stone house with black shutters and a red front door was welcoming, but we were both anxious. I tried really hard not to show my nerves, but the moment took my breath away. Here I was with a woman I didn't even know just nine months ago when she stood up and asked me a question after my speech, and now I was taking her to meet her daughter she had given up at the age of sixteen.

As we got out of the car, we could see the three of them opening the front door. Standing there was a beautiful young girl with round tortoiseshell glasses and a big smile. Her parents stood behind her, looking on protectively, showing support. Mr. Motley was in a suit and tie, even though it was a Saturday, and Mrs. Motley was in a print dress of navy and beige. They stood next to one another, with Joanne in front of them, their arms holding her. I started to tear up. I had a lump in my throat, the kind you feel when something really important is going on.

I took Ursula's hand, and we walked up to them. Joanne and Ursula hugged immediately and passionately, and both the Motleys and I stepped to the side after shaking hands. We all stood there. It felt very strange.

We went inside. The Motleys invited us into their kitchen where we sat on a lovely banquette and had iced tea and zucchini bread. Mrs. Motley was a gracious hostess. "Can I get you some more tea, Clair? Or zucchini bread? It's my great-grandmother's recipe. Joanne's favorite."

She made us feel very much at home. The conversation was a bit tense between Ursula and Joanne. "Joanne, how's school?" asked Ursula. "Do you like your classes? I bet you're a good student."

Joanne nodded her head but didn't say anything.

The resemblance was striking. They both had high cheek-bones and the same color deep hazel eyes.

After about ten minutes of small talk from Mr. Motley—"How was your drive in from the Main Line? Beautiful day, today"—he took over and got to what we were all thinking.

"Ursula," he said, lowering his head and then lifting it up, "we realize what a difficult situation you found yourself in sixteen years ago, and we would never judge you. We are indebted to you for giving us our precious Joanne. She has enriched our lives beyond words." At that, he reached for a neatly ironed stark white handkerchief he took from his pant pocket and gently dabbed his eyes. "We realize you gave birth to Joanne, and you deserve a place in her life for that reason." It was apparent they were very secure, kind people.

We stayed about half an hour, and then we all instinctively

knew it was time to go. Mrs. Motley made a big fuss over the bouquet of white roses, and we hugged when we left. When we got in the car, Ursula burst into tears, and I had to stop driving after we got around the corner from their home.

"My God, I never should have given her up!" she screeched. "I'm the lowest person on earth!" She wailed so hard I thought I might have to take her to the hospital. "I don't even deserve to see her, now, after what I did. I don't even deserve to live."

I tried to console her. "Ursula, you have done an amazing thing coming here and meeting your daughter. Can you see why many people don't? You have given your daughter a great gift. Don't you think she has wondered about you? Of course she has. Everyone wants to know their parents, even if they don't admit it. It's a natural thing to want to know."

She wasn't buying it. She threw her head against the window. "How can I ever make up for all the lost years? It's not possible. I shouldn't have come."

My heart broke for her. I held her tight. I think she just needed to get it all out. The emotion had been building for sixteen years. When she was able to calm down a bit, we drove home, and she went to sleep for a few hours. When she woke, the girls and I talked with her for a long time. It would be a day that will stay with me forever. We all have those days—the days when our lives turn on a dime. Unfortunately, I knew this too well. One thing I did know: I was bound forever with Ursula. That day she became my third daughter, and I was so grateful.

Two days later, the girls and I left for Turks. When we got to the airport, the private jet was waiting for us. When we got on board, the flight attendant got us settled in. It was a small plane, just about nine seats. The pilot came back and said hello, and in no time, we were up in the air. The girls had on their earphones and were on their iPads. They looked so grown up now. I thought back to the time we took them to Disney World when they were just four years old. I remember us walking around the park and suddenly Mickey Mouse appearing as we turned the corner. The girls went crazy—yelling, "Mickey, Mickey!" They stomped their feet in their pink sneakers and jumped up and down. I snapped a great photo of that moment, one of my favorites. I have it hanging in my laundry room, and I think of that fun time whenever I walk into the room.

And then my thoughts turned to Leon, as I leaned back and settled in. I couldn't wait to see him. Just as I was thinking about him and how wonderful it would feel to have him hold me in his arms, the flight attendant came by my seat and handed me a note. I could tell by my name written on the front that it was Leon's handwriting. I opened it, and it said, *Can't wait to see you. Would love to take you and the girls out on the boat tonight, that is, if you are up for it. Love, L.* My heart leaped. As wonderful as I felt, I still wasn't used to feeling so valued.

When Vince and I would wake up on a Saturday morning he would ask me what I was doing that day. And on Sundays when we were at the beach, he would leave bright and early to go biking with his club. It was pretty clear now that Kristee was the only member in the biking club. In a strange way, Leon's attention felt uncomfortable. Maybe it was more unfamiliar than uncomfortable. I hoped that I would get used to the feeling. I ran my finger over the ink of his words. I stared out the window. In just three hours I would be in paradise.

The girls slept the entire way, and I had to nudge them about fifteen minutes before we landed. When we walked off the plane, there was a car there for us, which Leon had arranged. Leon did things not to impress but because he loved doing nice things for people. That hadn't been the way with Vince. He was a big name dropper, and he loved medical doctors. Whenever we would meet someone in the medical field, he would always ask if they knew his internist, or his urologist, or his cardiologist. It was very strange. There was always a bit of *Godfather*-esque embellishment to his conversations with people. I just tolerated it at the time, but in looking back, I think it was symptomatic of his narcissism.

We got to our house, and the girls and I were thrilled to be there. Emilie opened the French doors to the beach and stood outside with her arms stretched to the sky. She said enthusiastically, "Yes! Yes!"

Reese followed right behind and shouted, "Yea, we're here!"

I asked them if they wanted to take up Leon's offer. They said they did, so I texted him that we were here and thanked him for the ride, both in the air and on land. He said he would come over at six and pick us up.

We had a few hours to ourselves. We decided to take a long walk on the beach, which felt so good. We stopped at Seven Stars and had an iced tea and watched the bathers enjoy the water. I told the girls to just stay in their bathing suits since everything was going to be very casual and very fun on Leon's yacht. And that's just what we did.

Leon appeared looking handsome as ever. He was most kind to the girls, giving them each a hug. When he hugged me, I could feel my body want to stay close, rather than letting go. My face touched his, and we kissed each other on the cheek. It was difficult not to greet him in the way I wanted to, but there would be time for that later. I knew the girls would be shocked when they saw his yacht, which they were, but I think it was good that I didn't make a big deal over it. I didn't want them to think that Leon was only about the stuff that he had because that was definitely not true.

It was a glorious night. Leon had the yacht packed with lots of good things to eat on board—lobsters, fine wine. It was the perfect beginning of great times for the four of us. The girls had a fun time, but most importantly, it was nice they were getting to know Leon—the Leon I had grown to love and care about in just the last few months; the Leon who wanted to know all about them—their hopes, dreams, and goals.

We all had experienced great tragedy, and we still had a lot to get through; but on this day, this spectacular day in Turks, life was good.

Chapter 27

We spent the next two weeks luxuriating in Turks—long walks on the beach, some intense tennis games, and lovely sunset sails. Ursula came for a week's vacation from work, and she very much wanted to go with us to Haiti, so we all agreed that it would be nice to have her along.

Leon arranged a charter flight to Port-au-Prince, which took a little over half an hour. He arranged for us to stay at the palatial Royal Oasis Hotel in Petionville, a suburban area about a half hour's drive from the airport. The hotel was built from investments from the Clinton Bush Haiti Fund. Leon felt it was the safest and the nicest of the hotels that were built after the earthquake. I had no idea what to expect, but I was eager to see the country, as well as learn about the work Leon had been doing there since January of 2010.

When we checked into the hotel, the staff was excited to see Leon, greeting him with hugs. They couldn't have been nicer, and it was readily apparent that Leon was held in high regard.

Obviously, he had stayed at the hotel often. Our rooms were very nice and modern in design with crisp white sheets and soft sheer white curtains on the windows that framed the mountains.

We had a quick lunch of rice, beans, and chicken, along with a bottle of water, and then headed out to see Leon's camp that he established for the children of the homeless earthquake victims. As we walked up to the entrance, after a bumpy ride in an old VW bus driven by a local Haitian with a big smile and missing teeth, there was a sign that read, *Ethan's Place*, which Leon named after his son. There was a guard standing outside the huge metal structure that had bars on the windows.

Once inside, it was like a scene from *The Wizard of Oz* when Dorothy landed in Oz and the film went from black and white to beautiful color. There were boys playing basketball at one end of the large space. There was a group of kids playing different instruments. There were girls taking ballet. There were kids doing art projects. There were children being tutored in math and English by volunteers. It was a happy place, and it was bustling with activity.

Leon had set up the foundation that funded the center. He was able to get donations from other Caribbean banks, set up a board, and hire an executive director. There were some local women cooking in the industrial-style kitchen with pots hanging from the ceiling, and they were laughing and having a great time.

I turned to Leon filled with emotion and said, "You really are amazing."

Of course, he replied, "I didn't do it all myself. I had a lot of help."

The girls and Ursula were very moved by Leon's work, as well. "Mom," said Reese, "I can't believe Leon did all of this."

After visiting upbeat Ethan's Place, we drove about ten minutes to the deplorable camp-type living situation where the earthquake survivors lived with their families. The families were still living in tents with unsanitary conditions. There were thousands of families.

The next two days involved meeting many of Leon's fellow volunteers who had shaped the rebuilding of Haiti. I was so impressed with the commitment of these people, and so were Emilie and Reese. I could see their former ideas of where they saw themselves in their future careers in medicine and law were changing. We were all changing.

When we left Haiti, we had a few more days in Turks before Ursula needed to return to the States. One morning Emilie and Reese slept in, and Leon, Ursula, and I took a long walk on the beach.

"Ursula," said Leon, as we walked hand in hand with Ursula next to him, "I'm happy you have reunited with your daughter. That was very courageous of you. I'm glad that you had a happy outcome."

"Well, it's a work in progress. It still feels strange, but I've been out to their home again, and things are getting a bit easier. At least I'm not an emotional mess any longer! I thank you so much for helping to make this all happen."

"Adoption is emotional and complicated. In my case, my birth mother worked for my parents as a domestic, so it was really strange when I was told that she was my birth mother. She had practically raised me. It wasn't until I was twelve that my adoptive parents sat me down and explained that my birth mother had gotten pregnant, and rather than giving the child up, she give me to them."

"Really? Wow, that's quite a story."

"Even crazier when my friends found out about it. I was ready to go to boarding school in London, and my parents felt I should know. Not sure if the timing was the best, but it was what it was," he said, adjusting his sunglasses.

I said nothing and was captivated by the story since Leon and I had never discussed it. I squeezed his hand tighter, as if to send a message that I loved hearing his story.

"But, Ursula, you did an amazing thing," he said. "Your daughter may be struggling with the surprising news and getting to know you, but in the end, I know it will benefit everyone—even the adoptive parents—although they might not realize it at the moment."

"How so?" she asked.

"Well, they probably knew the day would come when they would be faced with your coming upon the scene, and now that it is out in the open, things will fall into place and that worry is over for them."

"I see. Yes, you're probably right."

Leon's kindness was infectious. Since Ursula never had a male role model in her life, I knew that this conversation with Leon was important to her.

The next morning, I got up early. I sat on the patio with a cup of tea, watching the waves crash onto the sand. There was a text from Captain Martin to call him. He answered right away.

"Hello, Clair. How are things in Turks?"

"Divine," I said abruptly.

"I wanted to update you on things. Did I catch you at a good time?"

"I'm all ears."

"Detective Edwards and I got a chance to meet with Kristee."

I was trying to brace myself for what he was going to say.

"My goal after reading her rights was to set the stage for Detective Edwards to talk to her in a nurturing way about mistakes we have all made in our lives."

"What did she look like?"

"She looked fine, I suppose," he said.

"Fine? That's all?" I realized I must have sounded strange to Captain Martin, but I felt overwhelmed.

"Clair, my goal was to make her think about things for when she meets with her lawyer so she can realize that there is overwhelming evidence against her, so much so, that there is no way she can get away with this."

"And have her confess, right?"

"Well, yes, that's the plan. We want her to confess for a lesser sentence that Prosecutor Silver and her lawyer will work out."

"What's some of the overwhelming evidence?" I asked.

"Tom Coleada's revelations."

"Which are?" I wasn't only direct; I was rude.

"He's confessed to being paid by Kristee to kill Vince in order to get $500,000."

"My God, that's how much she paid him?"

"Yes, and he said the check was written from the company account."

"Jane didn't mention any check that stood out to her other than the one to CR Consulting."

"And who is Jane?"

"I hired a forensic accountant to go through everything."

"Well, he said the check was written the day she handed it to him on the tape."

"Just coincidental that the $500,000 check to CR Consulting was for the same amount?"

"We need to get a copy of the check that was written to Tom."

"My thoughts, exactly," I said. "Seems like an awful lot of money paid to Catherine Rogers for consulting work."

"Clair, are you feeling okay? You seem a bit distant."

"I'm just tired of the whole mess. Vince lied to me so much about money, who knows who got what? The way he covered things up, who knows what really happened."

"We'll figure it out. Just let us do our work. I'll keep you posted."

"Okay, but what did Kristee say? You didn't finish. Sorry I interrupted you."

"At first she didn't say anything other than she wasn't going to speak without her lawyer. Seems her parents have secured one of the big-time Philly lawyers, and he evidently told her not to say anything, which I understand. But when we left, she blurted out, 'I didn't kill Vince.'"

"And what about the gun? Who supplied that?" I asked.

"Tom said Kristee had given him the gun."

"Where is the gun now?"

"He said he threw it away in a dumpster in South Philly."

"All right. Thank you."

I got another call, so I got off quickly.

"Hello, Clair, it's Jim. Are you busy?"

"Oh, no, not at all, Jim. What's up?"

"Well, when we met the other day and you were asking me about Catherine Rogers and her company, CR Consulting, and the $500,000 check, I looked in Vince's file. He never wrote a check out to her to CR Consulting. She was on retainer for $20,000 a month that was paid to another company name she uses, Alchemy. Your accountant should see that."

"Is that so?"

"Yes. I thought you would want to know that."

"Yes. Thank you, Jim. Jim, one more thing: Can you please get me a copy of the check—front and back—that was for the $500,000 written on the day Vince was shot?

"Sure."

"Thanks."

I tried to reach Jane, but got her voice mail. I left a message:

"Jane, please look in the company ledger and tell me the number of the check written to CR Consulting. Thanks, Clair."

Chapter 28

I knew I needed to get home. Things were starting to materialize, and I felt uncomfortable being away. The girls and Leon agreed. We left two days later.

I had arranged a meeting with Captain Martin and Detective Edwards at their request, but before I met with them, I needed to go to Vince's office. Jim had texted me that he had a copy of the $500,000 check. I also wanted to talk with him about eventually selling the company. Now wasn't the time to delve into the subject, but I wanted to plant the seed. There was another steel wholesaler, actually a competitor of Vince's, in Chicago, whom Vince had mentioned from time to time, and I thought he might be a good fit.

And then there was an email from Jane: "The number of the $500,000 check to CR Consulting is written in the ledger as #2250. Hope this helps. Call me with anything else."

When I got to Vince's office, I walked down to Jim's office, and he was on the phone. He got off the call as soon as he saw me.

"Hi, Clair. How are you? How was Turks?"

"Very nice, Jim. So, do you have the check?"

"Yes. It's not written, however, to CR Consulting, and I'm not familiar with the name of the person to whom Vince made it payable."

I took the check from him and looked down at it. It was an almost-pulled-off version of Vince's handwriting, but the real telling factor was that it was written in blue ink. Vince only used black ink. He was adamant about it. And it was made out to Tom Coleada. "So why do you think that would be—that in the ledger it says one thing, but on the check, it says another?" I asked, playing dumb.

"Clair, I have no idea. Vince oftentimes did his thing and then told me about it later. Obviously, this was one of those times."

"Okay, I'll take it with me."

Because Tom had confessed that Kristee had paid him $500,000 and that the check for CR Consulting was for $500,000, I wasn't surprised they were the same check. Kristee apparently wrote CR Consulting in the ledger thinking that if anyone looked at the books, the person wouldn't question it. Even though it was what I had suspected, it still was shocking to see his name on the check. I felt numb but didn't want Jim to suspect anything further with the investigation still ongoing with Tom and Kristee. I tried not to look shocked at this revelation.

I said, "I also wanted to talk with you briefly about considering selling the business." I paused for a moment, but he showed no emotion. "I don't want to be involved with it any longer, and I know you don't have the financial capacity to buy me out, so I was thinking about Marcus Blackman."

"I know Vince liked him a lot and had a great deal of respect for him, even though they were fierce competitors."

"Those were the kind of people Vince liked and admired the

most," I said, smiling. "After all the other stuff in my life is settled, I'll contact him, if you are okay with it."

"Sure."

"All right, I just want to stop in Vince's office to take home some of his photographs."

"Yes, of course."

I walked into Vince's office and put a few of some great photos in my tote bag. There was one of him playing golf with Tiger Woods at Pebble Beach. He was most proud of that one. There were also some cute ones of him with the girls and some others of him with business people, but none of me, or him and me together. That should have been the real tip-off to his running around.

I was about to leave, and then something told me to open up one of his desk drawers. It was locked, but when I opened the top shallow drawer, I saw two small keys on a wire ring. I tried the first one, but it didn't open. But when I tried the other, it did. My eyes immediately gravitated to a file marked *Trips*. I opened it, and there were two tickets to Costa Rica for the same time I was to have been with the girls in Turks when he said he had to go to Brazil to look into buying the hardwood floor business. Not surprising, the names on the tickets were Vincent Bondi and Kristee Adams. I took the tickets with me. Maybe Detective Edwards would want them. I felt like I had been punched in the stomach. I felt like canceling the meeting with Captain Martin and Detective Edwards, but I knew I had to go.

I grabbed a quick yogurt at Wawa, and then I was on my way downtown. When I got to Captain Martin's office, I handed him the check. "Well, there you have it. Kristee obviously wrote out the check to Tom and then put CR Consulting in the ledger. It's the same check."

"Good work, Clair. You might want to work for us," he said

with a straight face, looking at the check. He then handed it to Detective Edwards.

"I'll pass this on to Prosecutor Silver," she said.

"We have a lot to tell you, as well." He folded his arms together and sat back on his chair. "Prosecutor Silver has met with Kristee's lawyer. She told him about all of our evidence—the tape from your detective of Kristee handing Tom the check, Tom's confession, as well as his tape at the convenience store impersonating a police officer. This is overwhelming evidence, but we still don't have a confession. And Silver wants a confession. She wants to offer time less served for a confession. She is recommending ten years for Kristee if she confesses. Without the confession, a trial will take place, and Tom will testify against her at the trial."

"And what about Tom's plea bargain? How much time is Prosecutor Silver recommending with all the stuff he has told us?"

"Twenty-five. He could have had life."

"When will we know if Kristee confesses?"

"Hopefully, soon. Let's get a victim impact statement ready to go from you to the judge. Keep it simple, just stating the impact of Vince's death has had on you and your daughters."

I left the station, thinking about what I would write for the victim impact statement, without saying that I was going to divorce Vince two days before he was shot. If all that had happened wasn't enough, Jane called.

"Clair, can you talk a minute?" she asked.

I was about to get my car at the parking garage, and I sat down on a bench outside the entrance. "Yes. But let me tell you first, the check is the same—$500,000. Kristee had to have written CR Consulting in the ledger, but when I got the check from Jim Stone today, it had been made out to and cashed by Tom Coleada."

"Incredible. Glad you found that part out. I have another part for you."

"And what's that?"

"I figured out by going through everything that both you and Vince received a yearly dividend from the company of $1 million. Vince deposited your dividend into the Turks account for the last eight years and he deposited his, as well as other monies from your developing business, into a building job in Florida that went bust."

"What building job?"

"It's called CWMI—Casa West Marco Island. I looked it up, and it seems like the same idea as Ocean Reef in Key Largo—an upscale compound-like community with lots of housing options on the water. Only the guy he was in with was a crook, to be quite frank, and he is actually serving time. He got in over his head— not Vince, the partner—and started doing some illegal stuff. Vince, unfortunately, put in a lot of money, and it was lost due to bad timing of the real estate market and the partner's misrepresentation of the financials of the business for loans. A lot of the money that you thought you had was absorbed by that investment."

"Well, as sad as that is, at least I now know where the money went." I wanted to keep my focus on getting justice for Vince's death, so nothing was going to bother me anymore.

Chapter 29

The timing was perfect for the sentencing hearing, right before the girls headed back for their last year of medical school and law school. We were all grateful that we didn't have to go to trial. I wanted Leon to be with us, but Prosecutor Silver told us to leave him at home.

"No photo ops or news stories about who the man was with you," she said.

There was a lot of media coverage, both locally and nationally. The courthouse was at capacity, and it was difficult to make our way in. We didn't say anything to the reporters, as Prosecutor Silver had told us. She also told us that she would do the talking after the sentencing hearing when we went outside. She suggested that we not be a part of that, which I hadn't intended on doing, but she said it was up to us.

Captain Martin and Detective Edwards sat beside me, and Emilie and Reese sat behind Prosecutor Silver. Kristee and Tom were seated in the front next to their respective attorneys. No one made eye contact. Kristee had on a white blouse and a navy-blue skirt, and her hair was pulled back into a bun. She was dressed much more conservatively than she normally dressed. Tom had on black slacks and a black shirt and black tie.

Since Captain Martin had explained to me that in almost all plea-bargain cases the judge takes the recommendation of the prosecutor, I was expecting to hear ten years for Kristee and twenty-five years for Tom. Captain Martin had explained the process: Prosecutor Silver would make a statement, followed by the judge asking Tom and Kristee if they had anything to say, and then they would give their remarks, if any, and then the sentencing.

"All rise for Honorable Judge Norma Cleary," announced the court clerk.

Prosecutor Silver, a small-framed woman who looked to be in her fifties, very plain with no makeup and short brown hair, stood before the court and emotionally began her statement.

"We have a very sad situation in which we find ourselves here today. Vincent J. Bondi was fatally shot by Tom Coleada and paid to do so by Mr. Bondi's assistant, Kristee Adams. As a result of the unspeakable, unconscionable actions of both Mr. Coleada and Ms. Adams, Mrs. Clair Bondi, married to Vincent Bondi for over twenty-five years, will never see her husband again. And Emilie and Reese Bondi, last year law and medical school students, will never see their father again. The only good news today is that both Mr. Coleada and Ms. Adams have confessed to their involvement—her arranging and paying out of the company business the $500,000 she gave to Mr. Coleada, and Mr. Coleada's pulling of the trigger while impersonating a police officer. A sentencing recommendation by both the defense and prosecution has been agreed upon and previously presented to the judge, as well as a victim impact statement from Mrs. Bondi."

"Thank you, Prosecutor Silver," said Judge Cleary. You could tell she had a great sense of style even with the black robe on. She was very attractive with thick black hair parted down the middle. Her nails were painted red, and she had on beautiful diamond stud earrings that sparkled from the bench. As she spoke and listened, she moved papers around that were set in front of her.

"And the defense for Mr. Coleada? Any statement from your client?"

"Yes, Your Honor," said Tom's attorney, a young man with round glasses. He looked like he was still in law school. "Mr. Coleada wishes to read a statement."

"Your Honor," he said, as he stood up and fumbled to get a folded piece of legal paper out of his pocket and began reading his statement while rubbing his neck behind his right ear, "I admit with remorse and apology to the Bondi family, most specifically to Mrs. Bondi and her daughters, that I accepted $500,000 from Kristee Adams to fatally shoot Mr. Bondi. I was wrong to have done it, and I regret all the pain and sorrow I have inflicted upon you. Thank you." He bowed his head and neatly folded the paper and put it back into his pocket.

"And the defense for Ms. Adams? Any statement from your client?"

"Yes, Your Honor," said Kristee's attorney, a middle-aged, well-dressed man with a firm voice.

Kristee stood up. She bowed her head, and then with tears streaming down her face, she said, "No one will ever know what I had to endure. For six years Vince told me he was going to leave his wife—his wife that he hated." She continued, "I did everything for him. I even had an abortion. I didn't want to, but he said there would be plenty of time for us to have our own family. But that was all a lie, an awful lie. I gave up my life for him. All my friends told me I was crazy to stay with him, that all his gifts, trips, and money for my house was all a con job and that he would never marry me." With that, she stared right at me. "You didn't love him the way I did. And that money was mine. He told me it was. And Miss California, yes, he was seeing her, too. He even cheated on me." And then, strangely, she added, "But I never told Tom to dress up like a police officer. He decided to do that himself."

"Do you have anything else you wish to say, Ms. Adams?" the judge asked.

"No." And then came the judge's ruling.

"All right then, I will begin with Mr. Coleada. Mr. Coleada, because I have seen you in my courtroom before, you obviously have not understood the importance of no longer committing crimes, particularly killing a person. But, because you have confessed and have been cooperative with the investigation as well as shown remorse for your unspeakable actions, I hereby sentence you to a prison term of twenty-five years without parole." Tom showed no emotion.

"And now for you, Ms. Adams. Your arranging of the murder of Mr. Vincent Bondi, a married man with whom you admittedly had an affair and who was also your boss, saddens me. I am also saddened that you saw no way out of the situation in which you found yourself other than to take money from the company to pay Mr. Coleada to fatally shoot Mr. Bondi. I appreciate your confession, but what I don't appreciate is your lack of remorse. I hereby sentence you to a prison term of fifteen years with the possibility of parole after serving a period of ten years. It is my hope that by that time you will have remorse for what you have done."

Kristee's mother, who was sitting with her father in the row behind her, burst into tears. Her father tried to console her, but she was hysterical and shouted out for all to hear: "I told her not to get involved with a married man, but she wouldn't listen." Her husband pulled her up from her seat and took her out of the courtroom. Kristee sat crying in her seat.

At that, the girls and I left the courtroom with Captain Martin and Detective Edwards. We quickly exited through a side door to Charles waiting for us in our car. We collapsed and fought back tears as we got into the back seat.

"Mom," said Emilie. "Dad got her pregnant. How low is that? Disgusting. I'm sick to even know he was my father." Reese said nothing, lowering her head and closing her eyes.

"It's all over now," I said, as I reached for each of their hands as mine trembled. "It's all over now, and we will get through this. We have one another."

Leon decided to give us our space and stayed at the Marriott that night. He wanted to be close in case I asked him to come over, but he was right: I needed to be with the girls. I couldn't stop thinking about what it must have been like when Kristee told Vince she was pregnant. I couldn't imagine their conversation. How different things might have been now if Kristee had insisted on having the baby. My daughters would have had a half brother or sister. I couldn't get my head around the thought of it. To think that all this was going on without my knowledge was unbelievable.

And I thought about when Kristee had come to my house to pay her respects with her co-worker and had brought a plant, and I had asked her about Catherine Rogers. She knew about their affair, and that was probably the tipping point that made her hire Tom Coleada.

As I lay in bed later that night, thoughts raced through my mind. I realized I would never know the real story of why Vince put the money—my part of the money—in Turks. Since he had started putting the money away two years before Kristee came to work for him, it didn't make sense that he put it there for her or for them. But there was one thing I did know: I wanted to begin work right away in setting up a foundation for single moms in North Philadelphia. I wanted to rehab their homes. A home was always central to my life—my being—and I knew the stability a home brought to a family.

And I wanted to meet Calvin Howard, the young man falsely accused of Vince's death. I couldn't think of anything worse to happen to a person than being accused of a crime he or she didn't commit. How could a person ever get back all those years?

I tried to close my eyes and fall asleep. When I looked at the clock, it was three in the morning, and I still hadn't dosed off. I heard footsteps in the hallway and saw Reese and Emilie walking downstairs. They weren't able to sleep either. When they saw I was up, they both came into my bed, and we hugged one another until they fell asleep.

As I held them close to me, I didn't know how I could ever make up for their pain.

Chapter 30

Moms Matter was formed the very next day. The foundation would serve single mothers in North Philadelphia who owned their homes by making their homes function and look better. Whether there was a leak that needed to be repaired, or a new hot water heater or oven needed, or just some fresh paint and new carpeting, Moms Matter would help. My goal was to get contractors and suppliers to donate their time and services. But little did I know that once all my wonderful subcontractors I used for my building and design business found out about it, they wanted to help. Donations started pouring in from individuals and corporations, as well.

I began by taking a block at a time. I found out who lived in each house, and if the owner fit the criteria, I was there to help. The women were shocked and so appreciative. I never got such satisfaction for an eight-burner Viking range I placed in a $9-million beach house as I did for a four-burner Kenmore stove. Water-stained walls were painted an array of bright Benjamin

Moore colors. Bare floors were covered in soft carpets. And Ben Johnson, my cabinet guy, installed cabinetry he would remove from his clients' homes that was still in good condition and place in theirs. With a fresh coat of paint, they looked brand new.

The streets came alive—landscapers donated their time and planted trees and shrubs; electricians installed outdoor lighting. Kids felt safe as they rode their bikes and played ball and board games under the streetlights. Neighbors spent more time outside and had block parties. Other neighbors became inspired and started taking better care of their homes. Financial experts began helping people not in the program get mortgages.

People were noticing. Mayor Nutter met with me, and city council gave me an award. When President Obama came to Philadelphia, he met with me, as well, and we walked the streets and saw the homes and visited with the mothers who were the recipients of my foundation's work. The moms squealed with joy from their front stoops and porches when they saw the dashing president.

After things got underway, I still hadn't met with Calvin Howard, the young man who had been falsely accused and held for Vince's death. He had been out of jail for about a year, and I still hadn't made the time to meet up with him. I had no idea where he was or where he lived, so I got in touch with Captain Martin, and he was able to find out. Calvin, unfortunately, was living on the streets. It was a huge problem in Philadelphia, even in fashionable Rittenhouse Square. Many homeless people slept on the benches of the square surrounded by multi-million-dollar apartments.

I was able to meet with Calvin, along with Captain Martin, in a small coffee shop in North Philadelphia. Since I had been in the area so much for my foundation, I knew the spot. Calvin was suspicious of our meeting, and I think for an instant he worried that he had done something wrong. Captain Martin let us talk, as he sat in a booth in the back of the restaurant and looked at his phone.

"Calvin, thank you for coming," I said.

"Everything okay?" he asked, with uncertainty.

"Calvin, I wanted to apologize for what happened to you."

"Why are you apologizing? You didn't do nothing wrong."

"I feel bad that you were held in jail for a crime you didn't commit."

"It happens to Black guys. You watch the news?"

"Yes, I do. And I understand." I didn't really understand because it was a world I had never been a part of, but I wanted to. "How are you doing?"

"I'm okay." He pulled down his red Phillies baseball cap closer to his eyes and squirmed in the booth. He had a tattoo on his arm that said, "Live, Die, Live." I wondered if he had it before he had been held for Vince's death or he had gotten it after. He seemed like he had difficulty sitting still, but maybe he was nervous.

"I hear that you're living on the streets."

"Yeah."

"I'd like to help you change that. Would you like a job?"

"A job? What could I do? I don't have no training or nothing."

"Yes, a job. I run a foundation that helps single moms with their homes right in this area. I could use your help."

He bowed his head and then looked up at me with his large brown eyes that conveyed a young man who had given up. "What could I do?"

My heart felt warm. He seemed like he would take me up on my offer, although he didn't know at this point what that offer was. "I need help with some cleaning up—sweeping, cleaning up after the contactors, seeing the trash is put out properly—things of that sort. You up for it?"

"Ah, maybe."

"Good." I thought I wouldn't say another word and would take him over to one of the houses right then and there. "Let's go. Come with me."

I left a twenty-dollar bill on the table, and we said goodbye to Captain Martin. Calvin and I got in my car and drove to a house I was working on.

"Nice," he said, when he saw the freshly painted house that stood out next to the shell of a home next door. Calvin began that day, that moment, helping out and getting paid. He always showed up and never let me down. It was this kind of moment, along with many others, that was changing my life's course.

Chapter 31

The next nine months flew by. The foundation was going great, and Reese and Emilie were about to graduate. Reese was going to do her residency in ob/gyn at Weill Cornell, so she would be moving to New York, and Emilie had accepted a position at a law firm in Los Angeles. They were swapping coasts. But before they started in the fall, they wanted to help out with the foundation. For the summer, they were both home with me, which was so very nice.

The mothers were very moved by their work. Reese talked to them about immunizations and nearby clinics, and Emilie talked about protection orders and places they could go for free legal help.

Leon was still in the picture, as he and I made our way back and forth from Philadelphia to Turks and Caicos. It never got old.

With all that was going on, I had left the steel business day-to-day workings to Jim, but I knew I had to end that. I never really knew, and possibly would never know, what Jim knew or didn't know about Kristee and Vince. At this point, it really didn't matter. What mattered is that I felt it was time to sell the business. I made the call to Marcus Blackman, and I went to Chicago to talk with him. He was a kind man and made me feel very welcome. He and his wife took me to lunch at the Ralph Lauren restaurant on Michigan Avenue. I felt like I could be friends with them, and we agreed we would all stay in touch. After a few months of negotiations with lawyers, a deal was struck. It was a huge relief. It was one more thing off my plate.

I also got back to developing another house at the beach. This was a smaller one than I had done in the past, and it was a renovation. I was excited to take a glorious house that was a pillar of gracious living at the beach back in the 1940s and bring it into the twenty-first century.

Leon and I had made plans with the girls to spend Christmas in Turks. The house was decorated beautifully with lights, wreaths, and a 12-foot spruce tree. We had breakfast on the terrace Christmas morning. We all said how grateful we all were to be together.

No sooner had I returned home after the New Year, I received a call from President Obama's chief of staff saying that Mr. Obama wanted to meet with me. I was shocked, to say the least. Of course I said I would and did so a week later. I had no idea, nor did the chief of staff give me any idea what the reason was for the meeting, but I was delighted to find out.

Unbelievably, President Obama wanted to appoint me to a project analyst position in the Department of Housing and Urban Development. He wanted me to set up Moms Matter in major cities throughout the United States. The job would be based in DC. I didn't hesitate for a moment and told him immediately that I would be honored to accept.

I called the girls and Leon as I walked out of the White House onto Pennsylvania Avenue. I got Reese first. "Reese, you will never believe this! The president wants me to set up my foundation in other cities!"

"Mom, that's amazing!" she boasted. I got the same response from Emilie and Leon. "Great job, Mom." "Clair, that is the best news ever!"

I stood on the corner looking down at the Capitol and just beamed with joy. I felt confident I had the right people working for the foundation in Philadelphia, which would allow me to move to DC and begin another part of my life.

As I took the train back to Philadelphia, my mind was racing. Sam LeVele could finish my building project at the beach, so that wouldn't be a problem. I would sell the Villanova house and talk to Leon about buying a home together in Georgetown. I wanted it to look just like the house of the television show *Madame Secretary*. I could already envision the black-painted grand mahogany banister to the second floor, and we would frequent all the fun places of Georgetown, such as Café Milano and Paolo's.

That all happened, and nearly two years later, I had Moms Matter set up in Los Angeles, Chicago, and New York City. I absolutely loved what I was doing. Leon came and met me for weekends in the cities where I was working at the time. My favorite was Chicago, where we regularly took the Architectural Boat Tour.

But I was taken off guard by a phone call from President Obama. "Clair Bondi, I need to give you an award for your great work helping out all those moms," he said. "Michelle and I would like to invite you and your family in January. You have made such a difference to those incredible women."

I immediately booked a room for Leon and me at the Four Seasons Hotel in Georgetown, since we were renovating our Georgetown house and we had to find another place to live for two weeks while the major work was being done. We were redoing all the bathrooms at the same time, so we couldn't stay there. I would see if the girls could make it but wasn't sure if they could. Leon was very interested and wanted to hear all about my conversation with the president and what was going to happen.

This was the culmination of my work. I never imagined all the good things that were happening. I was making an impact on the lives of women. But for some reason, my thoughts turned to Vince and his death. I had been so busy with the foundation and selling the steel business, plus moving to DC and the new appointment, that it had kept my thoughts and feelings about him at bay. Maybe I had not fully mourned his death. I started crying a lot and thinking about him in a revisionist manner. I remember my therapist telling me that people many times remember those who died in a better way than how the dead person actually treated them—like a widow who might have had an awful husband, but when he died, she extoled his virtues to a degree that was unrealistic. I didn't like how I was feeling. This was my time, and I didn't want to be thinking of Vince. I was angry with myself. I wondered if Vince would have been proud of me. But I didn't want to think about him. This wasn't about him; it was about me.

Chapter 32

The day of the award ceremony had arrived. While Leon ran out to get coffee, I wrote in my journal, something I had done every day since the age of twenty-five, although I hadn't written anything since the day Vince was killed. As I wrote that morning, I reflected on all that had happened. I felt relieved that I had tried my best to find out who was responsible for Vince's death; my girls deserved that. We needed to have closure. Strangely enough, I felt more settled, in control. It's crazy how change is the residue of heartbreak. If it weren't, we would all be stuck.

As I was getting ready, I took extra time to blow out my hair and apply my makeup. My black Prada dress and black heels seemed to do the trick because Leon couldn't take the smile off his face when I took a final victory twirl around the room.

"Ready, Clair?" he asked, as he put on his suit jacket. "This is your day!"

I didn't want to share how I really felt, so I just put on a happy face and said, "Yep! It's my day."

The driver arrived in a black Cadillac, and it was a short drive to the White House. Michelle Obama greeted us, which was so gracious of her. She looked stunning in a navy-blue knit dress and matching heels, but it was her intoxicating smile that stood out.

I thought she would be taking us to the Oval Office, but instead, we went into another room. When she opened the door, there, clapping and beaming, were my mom, Aunt Peg, Emilie and Reese, Barbara and Jack, and Ursula.

I turned to Leon and asked, "Oh, my God, how did this all happen?" He kissed me on the cheek. I knew he must have arranged for the special guests. I was overjoyed with pride and felt the love of everyone in the room.

And then President Obama greeted me with a warm smile and a hug and said, "Let's get started, shall we?"

As I stood next to the president while he introduced me and spoke of my foundation's work, I wanted to shout out from a megaphone and tell every woman looking for a better life that it could happen. If it happened to me under the very worst of circumstances, it could happen to them. I got lucky. I knew that, and I found it in such a sad way. How could my life be so good, so fulfilled now, in a way that it never had been before? I was in awe and shockingly amazed over the situation in which I found myself. I was helping hundreds of women with their homes, resulting in a better life for them and their children. My daughters were thriving—helping women with their legal and medical needs.

And then my eyes focused on Leon. We glanced at one another, tacitly solidifying our connection, and I thought back to the first time we met, when I turned and saw him walking from my house in Turks down to the beach to express his condolences for Vince's death. He stood by me from that very first meeting—helping me, caring for me, wanting the best for me, and encouraging me.

I wish I could have gotten from Vince what Leon had given

me—appreciation and respect. And now with Leon, my life, this *time* of my life, was different. Leon and I weren't doing the front nine; we were doing the back nine, and both were part of my journey.

With thanks and appreciation...

This journey began when my daughter Meredith Scardino suggested I attend a seminar her former New School professor and author Susan Shapiro was hosting at her Greenwich Village apartment. Meeting Sue changed my life, as she has done for so many of her students. No one can encourage, inspire, and make you dig down deep to your soul (painful!) to write your best piece more than Sue.

But really the path began with my degree from Temple University in journalism. Dr. Thomas Eveslage (communication law) and adjunct professors Linda Wright Moore (newswriting) and Walter Weir (advertising) were standouts. Temple's program is fantastic, and I so value my Temple experience.

And even before that was my dad, Charles L. Sacrey, who loved the written word and listened intently as I read him everything I had written during my formative school years. My deepest love and appreciation for my two siblings, William and Robert; William's partner, Charles Goldfine; my three stellar daughters,

Kim Scardino, Karen Scardino Strid, and Meredith Scardino; my terrific sons-in-law, Erik Strid and Andrew Sansone; and my fabulous grandchildren, Carter, Max, Olivia, Emma, and Oscar. And, as I mentioned in the dedication, all my love, respect, and gratitude for my mom, Emma Packett Sacrey.

Many thanks to those who assisted with content and connection—Jane Altschuler, Mary Stengel Austen, Len Bernstein, Tara Theune Davis, Leslie Ehrin, Andy Fisher, Emily Foote, Joe Hennessey, Leigh Himes, Louise Jones, Nellie Kurtzman, William Lashner, Ashley Lomery, Susan Muller, Helen Reese, Andrew Sansone, Kim Scardino, and Meredith Scardino.

Special thanks to kind supporters of this effort: Betty Bortz, Lisa Ferri, Meredith Foote, Susie Foote, Micah Hoffman, Catherine Kislowski, Jim Kittleman, Donna Litten, Rob Lopardo, Salli Mickelberg, Jan Pecarsky, Mary Rhoads, Carmen Richter, Louis Ruvolo, Kitty Smith, Caroline Waxler, Connie Willison, and Dona Duncan Wolfe.

Joy and happiness for my lifetime and supportive best friend, Barbara Chorley Tarditi, who sent me a quote by Nora Ephron: "Above all, be the heroine of your life, not the victim."

And finally, how ironic that it was a contact through my long-time association with the Philadelphia Ronald McDonald House who connected me with Naren Aryal, Jess Cohn, and Nicole Hall of Mascot Books. Eternal gratitude to author Marnie Schneider, board member of the Charlotte Ronald McDonald House. We share a love for helping the families of seriously ill children. I can't think of anything more important.

Anne Scardino, building and design consultant-turned-novelist, has always had a passion for writing, whether it be social commentary or design and travel. But it is her twenty-three years of volunteering at the Philadelphia Ronald McDonald House that has fed her soul. Anne holds a degree in journalism from Temple University and has taken coursework at Moore College of Art and Design and The New School. An avid fan of music and travel, Anne resides in Philadelphia. Her favorite place is Turks and Caicos.